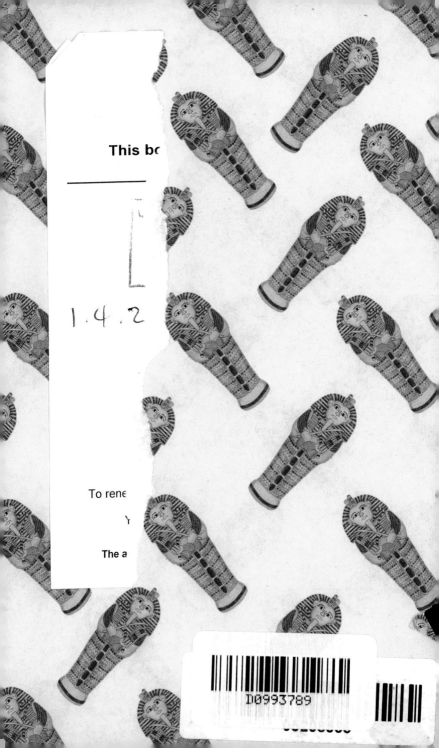

This bo

1.4.2

To rene

y

The a

THE INCREDIBLE SHRINKING GIRL absolutely Loves Ancient EGYPT

LOU KUENZLER was brought up on a remote sheep farm on the edge of Dartmoor. After a childhood of sheep, ponies, chickens and dogs, Lou moved to Northern Ireland to study theatre. She went on to work professionally as a theatre director, university drama lecturer and workshop leader in communities, schools and colleges. Lou now teaches adults and children how to write stories and is lucky enough to write her own books, too. She has written children's rhymes, plays and novels as well as stories for CBeebies. Lou lives in London with her family, two cats and a dog.

www.loukuenzler.com

THE INCREDIBLE SHRINKING GIRL

absolutely Loves Ancient EGYPT

LOU KUENZLER

Illustrated by Kirsten Collier

■SCHOLASTIC

Scholastic Children's Books
An imprint of Scholastic Ltd
Euston House, 24 Eversholt Street, London, NW1 1DB, UK
Registered office: Westfield Road, Southam, Warwickshire, CV47 0RA
SCHOLASTIC and associated logos are trademarks and/or
registered trademarks of Scholastic Inc.

First published in the UK as *Shrinking Violet Absolutely Loves Ancient Egypt*
by Scholastic Ltd, 2014
This edition published 2018

ISBN 978 1407 18782 2

A CIP catalogue record for this book
is available from the British Library.

Printed by CPI Group (UK) Ltd, Croydon, CR0 4YY
Papers used by Scholastic Children's Books are made
from wood grown in sustainable forests.

1 3 5 7 9 10 8 6 4 2

www.scholastic.co.uk

To the British Museum –

for being there! LK

CHAPTER 1

My name is Violet Potts.

This story begins as I was trying to solve a brain-ticklingly tricky wordsearch. It was the Competition of the Week in *SOLVE IT!*, my gran's favourite puzzle magazine. There were supposed to be ten hidden words all about Ancient Egypt.

"This puzzle is as tough as a mummy's toenail," I groaned, taking a **SLURP** of the hot blackcurrant drink Gran had made for me. I

1

was visiting her at the Sunset Retirement Centre, where she lives.

"The prize-winning ones are always tricky," said Gran.

Gran is TOTALLY puzzle crazy and I've done loads of crosswords and wordsearches with her before. But this one was impossible. There were pictures of birds, cats and sacred scarab beetles all down the side of the page. I knew these were hieroglyphs, or Ancient Egyptian writing. But there was no list of the hidden words we were meant to find or any clues to guide us.

"We're not doing *too* badly," said Gran. "We've found eight words already, I think."

I counted. She was right. We had:

Mummy
Tomb
Pharaoh
Pyramid
Papyrus
Hieroglyph
Scarab beetle
and River Nile.

"Look," cried Gran suddenly. "There's 'sarcophagus', right underneath 'scarab beetle'."

"Oh yes," I groaned, annoyed I hadn't spotted that one.

We had studied Ancient Egypt at school, so I knew a sarcophagus is like an Ancient Egyptian coffin. We had to do a special project and I wrote a gory diary of a mummy-maker. It was totally gruesome. Do you know they used to poke the dead person's brain out with a hook? My best friend Nisha said it made her feel sick.

"Isn't it funny with wordsearches, Gran?" I said as I ran a bright purple highlighter through the letters of 'sarcophagus'. "The minute you see a word, you can't believe you missed it."

"Life's a bit like that sometimes," laughed

Gran. "People don't see what's right under their own noses."

"I suppose so," I said. But I wasn't really listening. "Look," I cried, pointing to what was right underneath *our* noses. "If we find all the words, there's a really amazing prize."

I read out the information printed just below the puzzle. "**Win an all-expenses-paid cruise down the Nile and take part in an archaeological dig at a real Ancient Egyptian temple**."

"I only ever do the puzzles for fun," said Gran. "Hundreds of people must send in the right answers. I expect they just pick one out of a hat."

"But you have to do a tie-breaker too," I said, reading on. "Listen: **finish the following**

sentence in no more than ten words to help us find the best winner."

Gran looked at where I was pointing. "**I should win a trip to discover the wonders of Ancient Egypt because. . .**"

". . .*because* my school project was AMAZING and GORY!" I cheered.

Gran raised her eyebrows. "I don't know if that'll convince them," she said. "I think you're supposed to make a joke or something. Not that it matters anyway. We still haven't found the tenth hidden word."

"Tutankhamun?" I said hopefully. "He was a famous boy pharaoh."

"I think we'd have noticed a long word like that," said Gran.

"I suppose so," I agreed as we stared at the page.

"Tut," I gasped.

"Tut-tut," agreed Gran. "It *is* frustrating. . ."

"No," I cried, jabbing my finger at the puzzle. "Here. T–U–T spells 'Tut'. As in 'King Tut' – that's what they call Tutankhamun for short."

"Well, I never," said Gran. "No wonder we didn't see such a tiny word tucked away in the corner there."

She took the stubby highlighter and marked the three letters in purple.

"Gran," I said, grabbing her arm. "*I miss my mummy. . .*"

"Really?" Gran looked worried. "If you want to go home now, you can."

"No." I giggled. "You know I love being here with you. It's my answer to the tie-breaker, silly. Listen: **I should win a trip to discover the wonders of Ancient Egypt because . . .** I miss my mummy."

"Ha!" Gran started to giggle until her shoulders shook. "I get it . . . I miss my mummy! Like an *Egyptian* mummy. That's actually pretty funny, Violet. A little corny but. . ."

"It's BRILLIANT," I said. "Pack your bags, Gran. We're off to Egypt. With a line like that we're sure to w . . . w . . . WHOA!"

My toes had started to tingle.

I knew this feeling all too well.

"Don't get your hopes up," said Gran. "I shouldn't think they even read all the entries and. . ." She looked up from the puzzle. "Are you all right? Violet. . .?"

"Not exactly," I cried, clinging to arm of Gran's chair. The tingling in my toes had moved past my knees. "I'm SHRINKING. . ."

"Careful!" Gran's hands shot out as I tumbled forward.

PING!

The edge of the chair, Gran's knee, a plug socket in the wall all **whooshed** past me in a blur.

"Got you," cried Gran, catching me like I was a falling leaf, a moment before I hit the ground.

"Oops!" I grinned. "That was a close one."

Gran opened her fingers. I was so tiny, I was standing on her outstretched palm. I had shrunk to exactly the same size as the little purple marker pen she was holding in her other hand.

"Honestly, Violet." Gran's eyes were twinkling with laughter. "You should know better than to get in a fizz like that. Especially over a silly old puzzle. You know you shrink when you get yourself overexcited."

She didn't even look surprised. She knows my little secret. I've shrunk lots of times before. Gran used to be just the same when she was a girl. Back then, she was a shrinker too.

"Do you think we might actually win the competition?" I asked as Gran lifted me close to her ear so she could hear my tiny voice.

"I'D LOVE TO GO ON A TRIP DOWN THE RIVER NILE. WOULDN'T YOU?" I bellowed.

CHAPTER 2

Gran was right ... I should never have got so excited.

I grew back to full size after just a couple of hours but it was silly to have got my hopes up in the first place. A whole week went by and, even though I phoned Gran every day, there was still no news from *SOLVE IT!*. I'd been TOTALLY convinced they'd get in touch to tell us we were the winners.

"Are you *sure* you posted our entry?" I asked Gran when I telephoned her that Friday night.

"Honestly," sighed Mum, wagging her finger

at me across the kitchen table. "You've asked poor Gran that same question five times already this week."

"You never know, Mum," I whispered, putting my hand over the receiver. "Old people can be a bit forgetful. . ."

"Violet Potts!" Gran's voice boomed down the line. "I might be old but I am *not* forgetful. And I am not deaf either. If you are going to talk about me, you'll have to whisper a lot quieter than that."

"Sorry, Gran." I blushed. She had a point. I have never known Gran to forget anything – she says all those puzzles help keep her brain sparky. Although she's old, she's one of the liveliest people I know. That's why we get on so well. We're always looking for our next amazing adventure.

"It's a pity you think I'm so forgetful," she chuckled. "I seem to have forgotten the exciting news I had to tell you. . ." It was obvious she was going to make me suffer. "What was it now. . .?"

"Gran," I begged. "*Please* tell me."

"It not about the *SOLVE IT!* competition," she said quickly. "I really haven't heard anything about that." I could tell Gran was worried that if I got too excited, I'd shrink in front of Mum.

The rest of my family have no idea about my little shrinking secret. The very first time I shrank, I tried to tell them – several times – when I grew back to full size. We were at a theme park. But Mum and Dad just got cross and said I was making things up. That's when Gran explained it might be better to keep it to ourselves. She's right, of course. Mum would get in a terrible panic if she knew. She already worries that I don't eat enough fruit and veg. She worries that I ride my bike too fast. And she worries that I climb trees too high . . . go to bed too late . . . brush my teeth too quickly. It would definitely not be a good idea to add shrinking to the size of a lollipop to her **LONG** list of worries.

"How do you spell 'hieroglyph'?" said Gran from the other end of the phone.

"Why? Is it a crossword answer?" I asked.

"No – I just think it would be a very good idea if you tried to spell it for me," said Gran.

"Ah," I said, catching on at last. Gran knows that boring things like spelling – or disgusting things like eating Mum's spinach and broad bean bake – are always a great way to make sure I don't

get overexcited and shrink.

"You just spell," said Gran, "and I'll tell you

my plan."

"OK – hieroglyph," I began. "That's H …

erm." I really wasn't sure what came next.

"H-E…? H-I…? H-Y…?"

"How would you like to go to London

tomorrow?" said Gran. "I don't suppose we're

really going to win that trip to Egypt, so the

British Museum is the next best thing. They have

a huge ANCIENT EGYPTIAN collection. They've

got mummies and jewellery and statues and real

hieroglyphs too."

"That would be fandabbydosey," I cheered,

taking huge yucky bite out of a raw cabbage leaf

that was lying on the kitchen worktop. "F-A-N-D-A-B-B-Y-D-O-S-E-Y."

That evening I stood on tiptoe, looking into one of the million mirrors that hang on Tiffany's – my terrible teenage sister's – side of our bedroom.

I was holding a thick toilet roll in one hand and the long dangling end of it in the other. I turned slowly in a circle, trying to wrap the paper around my legs.

"Violet, what are you doing?" roared Tiffany, coming through the door. "Why have you crossed *The Line*?"

"The Line" is an old dressing gown cord which Tiffany pinned to the floor to keep me out of her side of the room.

"What does it look like I'm doing?" I said, tripping over the end of the toilet roll and falling into a heap on her bed. "I'm trying to dress up as an ANCIENT EGYPTIAN mummy, of course."

"Dressing up? You're such a baby," sighed Tiffany, grabbing me by my feet and trying to pull me back to my side of the room.

"You dress up in miniskirts and shoes you can't even walk in," I yelped. But as Tiff tugged me across the floor, I realized I was going about this all the wrong way.

"Tiffy?" I said, super sweetly, sounding like the cutest, most helpless little sister in the whole world. "Won't you help me, Tiffy? Please."

"No." Tiffany didn't bat a long, mascaraed eyelash as she dropped me on my side of The Line

17

and turned back to look at herself in the mirror. "Why should I help you?"

"Because it will be fun?" I tried. But Tiff just snorted. That's her trouble. She has no imagination. "If you help me, I'll give you an **ANCIENT EGYPTIAN** beauty tip," I said, thinking fast. I coughed and put on a deep, mysterious, fortune-teller sort of voice. "I will reveal the precious secrets of skin as smooth as marble. . ."

"Fine." Tiffany turned towards me with her hands on her hips. I knew that would get her attention. She spends hours in front of her million mirrors huffing and puffing if she has even the tiniest spot. . . Today she had a huge pink one, shining like a Christmas light, right in the middle of her forehead.

"Nile mud," I said simply. "Everyone knows it's good for your skin."

The only person I had ever actually heard say that Nile goo was the best sort of mud to squish on your face was Barry Bling, the horrible beautician who used to do treatments for Gran and the other old ladies at the Sunset Retirement Centre. Knowing Barry, he probably made it up.

"Nile mud?" gawped Tiffany.

"Yes," I smiled. "Just rub it on your face, relax for half an hour and *zing*!

"Where am I supposed to get Nile mud from?" groaned Tiff.

"The Nile?" I shrugged. "A deal is a deal. I gave you the beauty tip, now you have to wrap me up."

"You haven't even got any bandages," said Tiffany. "That's just a toilet roll."

See what I mean? No imagination.

"Please, Tiff," I begged. "I'll dig you some mud from the garden later. I'm sure that will be just as good as the real thing."

"Fine," she sighed and began to wind the toilet roll around my ankles. "What I don't understand is why you want to look like a mummy in the first place?"

"I thought you could take a funny picture on your phone and text it to Gran," I explained. "To thank her for taking me to the British Museum tomorrow."

"If I was going to London, I'd head straight for the shops," said Tiffany. "What's the point in spending the whole day in a stupid museum?"

"The museum is not stupid. It's awesome," I said. "They have real-life mummies. . . Well, real *dead* ones, anyway."

"That's disgusting," said Tiff.

"Whoooo!" I giggled, peering into the mirror. I had to admit, Tiff had done a pretty good job of wrapping me up.

The toilet roll was wound all the way up over my head, just leaving a gap for my eyes and mouth.

It would have made a perfect picture, except just then Chip – my scruffy, naughty little dog – came BOUNDING into the room.

"Grrr!" he growled at the sight of me looking like a spooky mummy. He grabbed a loose corner of toilet roll and shook his head, yapping and throwing mouthfuls of paper all around Tiffany's side of the room. It looked as if a toilet-roll tornado had blown across her bed.

"Out!" screamed Tiffany as Chip and I fled for the door. The CURSE of an Egyptian mummy may be scary . . . but Tiff in a tantrum is far worse.

CHAPTER 3

By ten o'clock next morning, Gran and I were sitting on the top deck of a big red London bus.

I peered out of the window as crowds of people bustled along the busy pavement below us, jostling past each other with shopping bags, briefcases and baby buggies.

"Imagine **SHRINKING** on a street like that," I whispered. "Just think of all those feet. I'd be *SQUASHED* flat as a pancake ... if I wasn't eaten by a pigeon first."

"Don't even joke about it," Gran shuddered. "We'll have no shrinking today, Violet Potts."

"Don't worry." I opened my bag and showed Gran a little plastic sandwich box. "There are six pickled gherkins in there," I explained. "They're really vinegary, with a horrible super-sour tang."

"Ooh." Gran held out her hand. "I love pickled gherkins."

"I hate them," I said, lifting the box out of her reach. "That's the point. The minute I feel excited, I'll eat one whole. The taste is so totally disgusting, I won't be able to think about anything else. And I won't shrink."

"Good plan," laughed Gran. "Better wave one under your nose now. This is our stop."

We clambered down the stairs and jumped off the bus.

"There's the British Museum," said Gran, pointing to a huge building with tall stone pillars.

"It's so big," I gasped, popping a whole pickled gherkin in my mouth. "Yuck! Good job these taste so horrible or I'd be the size of an Ancient Egyptian *shabti* already." I shuddered.

"What's a *shabti*?" asked Gran.

"Follow me and I'll show you," I said.

Gran and I peered into a big glass case. We were staring at a row of tiny blue stone people, each about as tall as a clothes peg.

"So these are *shabti*," whispered Gran.

"What amazing little things. You're right, they're exactly the same size you are when you shrink."

"That's why I wanted to show you," I said. "The Egyptians used to put them in their coffins alongside the mummies."

"Perhaps they knew all about shrinking back then," Gran whispered.

Before I could answer, a plump man with a huge cowboy hat squeezed in between us. The brim of his hat was pulled right down over his face. All I could see was a long, droopy moustache poking out from underneath.

"Cute little guys, ain't they?" said the man, in an American accent. He tapped the case as if the tiny blue stone figures were lizards sleeping at a zoo. "What do you suppose they are? Some kinda mummified pixies?"

"They're called *shabti* actually," I explained. I had read all about them in my *Bumper Book of Ancient Egypt*.

"I can see you're a real smart cookie," said the man, slapping me on the back. "A regular little Egypt-o-whatnot. You know, like a professor or something."

"Egyptologist?" smiled Gran. "Violet did study the Ancient Egyptians for a project at school."

"Well, ain't that something. Pleased to meet you, Miss Violet." The man stuck out his hand and I shook it.

"And what's your name?" asked Gran, after she had introduced herself.

"Me? Er ... Tutankhamun," the man mumbled.

"Tutankhamun?" I tried not to giggle. "You mean like the famous Egyptian pharaoh?"

"No, Miss Violet. You must have misheard me."

He coughed. "The name's . . . Moon. Mr Carl Moon."

"Nice to meet you, Mr Moon," said Gran – though I would have bet two hundred of my favourite **Toffamel** bars he had said Tutankhamun the first time. Perhaps it was some kind of joke or something.

"Tell me, Miss Violet," he said, waving a guidebook under my nose, "what else has this place got from Ancient Egypt that I ought to see?"

"There's a brilliant mummified crocodile," I said. "And I'm looking forward to the cats."

"Cats?" Mr Moon twiddled the end of his moustache. "That does sound interesting."

"Oh!" laughed Gran as Mr Moon took her arm. "Come on then, Violet . . . I mean, Miss Violet. You lead the way!"

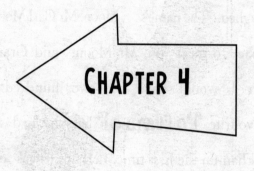

CHAPTER 4

"Cats were sacred in Ancient Egypt," I said as we stood looking at a poor old puss that had been turned into a mummy thousands of years ago.

The bandages were brown and crispy looking, like a very old parcel. Even the cat's little pointy ears had been wrapped up.

"Well, ain't that extraordinary?" said Mr Moon, pressing his nose up against the glass. "Thank you for showing me these, Miss Violet."

"No problem," I nodded.

I was distracted by a notice next to the case.

"How horrible," I gasped. "Listen to this: *Many mummified cats did not die a natural death. They were often sacrificed and offered as gifts for the gods.*"

"Poor things. I wouldn't have liked to be an Ancient Egyptian pussycat," said Gran.

"It's just awful," I agreed. Even though it had

happened so long ago, the thought of those poor cats gave me the creeps.

Mr Moon had tilted up the brim of his hat and was reading the notice for himself.

"Well, I never. Now that really *is* interesting," he said. Then he clicked the heels of his cowboy boots and bowed. "Better get going, ladies. Have a nice day."

And with that, he hurried off, leaving Gran and me to explore the rest of the exhibition by ourselves.

"What a funny man," I whispered.

"But very friendly," smiled Gran.

We had stopped in front of a brightly painted golden sarcophagus.

"Imagine how exciting it would be if you

were an archaeologist and you dug up one of these magnificent treasures," said Gran.

"If only we'd won the competition in *SOLVE IT!*. Then we could've had a go at being archaeologists ourselves," I sighed. "They said we'd be able to dig in a real Egyptian temple, remember?"

"We should forget all about that. We'd have heard by now if we'd won," said Gran, shaking her head – though I knew she'd been thinking exactly the same thing. "Come on. Let's go to the gift shop and I'll buy you a souvenir."

"As long as it's not a MUMMIFIED CAT," I laughed.

We linked arms and walked across the huge marble entrance hall towards the shop.

"And I want to find a postcard to send to your

cousin Anthony in Australia," said Gran.

I'd only met my cousin Anthony once, when we were both babies. I know it makes Gran sad his family live so far away. They hardly ever get to visit.

"See if there's a postcard of the mummified croc," I suggested. "There are loads of crocodiles in Australia, so I bet Anthony would like that."

I thought how brilliant it would be to have a boy cousin my own age to play with, instead of just Tiff. I'm sure Anthony wouldn't think dressing up like a mummy was stupid.

"Great idea," said Gran, flicking through the postcards. "You go and choose a little something for yourself. My treat."

"Thank you," I called as I hurried over to the

34

Egyptian gift section.

I had just chosen a key ring of a mummy all wrapped up in bandages, when I spotted Mr Moon again. He was in the kid's reading area, flicking through a copy of *The Bumper Book of Ancient Egypt*.

"I've got that one at home," I said, walking over to him. "It's great. It tells you everything you've ever wanted to know."

"Perfect, Miss Violet. That's exactly what I'm after," said Mr Moon.

He clutched the book as if it was an ancient treasure and hurried towards the till.

An hour later Gran and I were on the train heading home to Swanchester.

I was reading a FABULOUS PHARAOH FACT SHEET from the museum and Gran was doing a crossword. She'd picked up the latest copy of *SOLVE IT!* from the newsagent at the station before we caught the train.

Suddenly, I heard a weird GULPING noise. I looked up and saw Gran opening and closing her mouth like a goldfish.

"Quick. Chew this," she said, flicking the lid off my pot of pickled gherkins and shoving a whole one into my mouth. "Keep calm, Violet. You must keep *very* calm."

Out of the corner of my eye, I saw a businessman on the table across the aisle looking over at us.

"What is it, Gran?" I mumbled, through

a mouthful of gherkin. "I'm not excited, I promise."

"Ah, but you will be." Gran slid the copy of *SOLVE IT!* towards me.

I looked down at where she was pointing.

CONGRATULATIONS to the lucky winner of our Competition of the Week (Number 129), Mrs V. Short of the Sunset Retirement Centre, Swanchester. . .

"Mrs Short? But that's you, Gran," I spluttered, spurting vinegar all over the table. "I thought you said we hadn't won. . ."

"Read on," ordered Gran, tapping the page with her finger and waving another enormous gherkin in front of my mouth.

After answering the wordsearch correctly and sending in a hilarious tie-breaker, Mrs Short has won a family trip for four people to sail down the Nile and take part in a genuine, treasure-finding Ancient Egyptian archaeological dig.

"Pack your suncream, Violet," cried Gran. "Because. . ."

"We're off to Egypt!" I cheered as Gran leant across the table and threw her arms around my neck.

"Congratulations," said the businessman. "That sounds like quite a trip."

I must not shrink, I told myself, hugging Gran as tight as I could. If I did, the businessman would see me disappear in front of his eyes. But my heart was pounding with excitement.

"Who will you take with you, Gran?" I asked.

"My three grandchildren, of course," she grinned. "You … because without you we'd never have won the prize … and Tiffany and Anthony as well."

"Anthony?" I gasped. I was almost as excited that I'd get to meet my Australian cousin again as I was about the trip to Egypt. "Yippee!" I cried.

Luckily, the train pulled into the next station just at that moment, and the businessman got up to leave. If he had stayed for one second longer, he would have seen me SHRINK to the size of a train ticket and cartwheel across the table in delight.

"Egypt here we come!" I squealed as Gran scooped

me up and popped me in her pocket.

CHAPTER 5

Mum was not at all sure that the trip was a good idea.

"What do you think?" she asked Nurse Bridget, who looks after Gran at the Sunset Retirement Centre. "It just doesn't seem sensible for an old lady to take three children on a crazy adventure up the River Nile."

"I don't see why not," Nurse Bridget smiled. "Mrs Short has bags of energy and the doctor has given her the all-clear."

"If she slips and twists her ankle, she can always borrow a bandage from one of the mummies," laughed Dad.

"For goodness' sake, Stuart, this is no joking matter," sighed Mum.

"Gran's so fit she could *swim* the River Nile, let alone travel up it in a boat," I said.

"It's all set anyway," said Gran, before Mum could argue more. "I've organized the tickets with the competition department at *SOLVE IT!* Tiffany, Violet and I will meet Anthony at the airport in Cairo. His flight from Australia is due to land just half an hour after ours."

"It seems a long way for him to come just to look at some dusty old ruins," said Mum.

Gran raised her eyebrows.

"Honestly, Mum. We're not just going to *look* at the ruins. We're going to be actual **proper** archaeologists, digging in the desert sands," I cried, clapping my hands.

"The only digging I'm going to do," said Tiffany, "is to find fresh river mud for my face mask."

Oh dear. Perhaps I should never have told Tiff that Nile *SLUDGE* is good for the skin. If it wasn't for that, she probably wouldn't even have wanted to come on the trip in the first place and she could have stayed home, brushing her hair in the mirror, where she'd be much happier anyway.

At least Anthony was going to be more fun. I'd emailed him as soon as Gran found out we'd won the trip and we'd been sending each other messages every day since, saying how excited we were.

From: antsmall@ozsend.com
To: violetp@yippee.uk
Hi Violet
The awesome croc postcard from the British Museum arrived today. I reckon the Ancient Egyptians mummified just about anything that moved. . .
Wouldn't it be amazing if we found a real mummy on the dig?
Cousin Ant

From: violetp@yippee.uk
To: antsmall@ozsend.com
Dear Ant
Six days to go! Can't wait.
We're going to visit all the big tourist sites.

First, the pyramids and the

Valley of the Kings – then we meet the rest

of our tour group and catch a boat down the

River Nile to our archaeological dig.

It is going to be TOTALLY, TOTALLY TERRIFIC!

Violet

From: antsmall@ozsend.com

To: violetp@yippee.uk

Hi Violet

Five days to go!

I can't wait for the dig. It's going to be

the best bit of the trip. I want to be an

Egyptologist when I grow up. How about you?

From Ant

From: violetp@yippee.uk

To: antsmall@ozsend.com

Dear Ant

Being an Egyptologist would be super cool. I

would definitely like to do that – if I'm not a

stunt rider or a lion tamer. . . Or a theme park

ride designer.

Fingers crossed we find some real

treasure . . . or something extra-specially

gory. Woooo!

Four days to go!

From Violet

I waited for Anthony to reply. But his emails

suddenly stopped coming. I kept on writing every day.

From: violetp@yippee.uk

To: antsmall@ozsend.com

Hey Ant

Are you there? Hope you haven't been struck

down by a mummy's curse?

V.

But no answer came.

"He's probably just nervous about flying on

his own," said Mum when I told her Anthony had been silent for so long.

Hmm. That still doesn't explain why he is ignoring my emails, I thought. But at the mention of flying my heart started fluttering too. I'd been so busy thinking about Egypt and meeting Anthony I hadn't thought much about the journey. I couldn't wait to fly in a jumbo jet ... but imagine if I shrank before we even left the airport?

This calls for desperate measures, I thought.

I clipped my mummy key ring to the little backpack I was going to take on board the plane, then I sneaked down to the kitchen and packed a BUMPER-SIZE jar of pickled gherkins.

"Better not shrink when I'm going through customs," I shuddered to myself. "I'd show up on the X-ray machine as clearly as a smuggled diamond."

CHAPTER 6

In the end I had to survive without my pickled gherkins on the flight.

"No liquids in your hand luggage," the lady at the check-in desk explained.

"You don't even like gherkins. Or vinegar," said Tiffany. "What did you want to do? Pickle your own Egyptian mummy?"

"That would be pretty cool." I smiled, but I had to leave the pickles sitting on the top of a litter bin as we moved through customs.

I was so busy looking back at the abandoned

jar, I almost forgot to wave goodbye to Mum and Dad, who were smiling anxiously through the glass.

"See you soon," I called, a lurch in my stomach making me realize this was real. Tiffany, Gran and I were actually on our way.

All through the long flight to Egypt, I recited my seven times table and finally learned to spell hieroglyph. Forwards: H-I-E-R-O-G-L-Y-P-H . . . and backwards: H-P-Y-L-G-O-R-E-I-H. And sarcophagus too. Forwards: S-A-R-C-O-P-H-A-G-U-S . . . and backwards: S-U-G-A-H-P-O-C-R-A-S.

Tiffany filed her nails and chewed gum. She might as well have been sitting in the back of a car rather than flying on a plane for all the excitement she showed.

I looked out of the window and pinched myself as yellow desert sand came into view.

"Whatever happens I have to keep calm," I murmured as the plane landed and we walked across the tarmac towards the airport building. A blast of warm air hit me like a hairdryer.

"You're doing brilliantly," said Gran, squeezing my arm as we headed to the arrivals area to collect our cases from the luggage belt.

Tiffany couldn't hear us. She had headphones in and was paying no attention to what was going on around her.

As my ears POPPED from being back on the ground, I listened to excited voices calling out to each other in Arabic. Businessmen in long white robes were shouting into their mobile phones. Beyond the windows of the airport I could see the skyscrapers of the city but also palm trees and sandy rocks.

"I can't believe it," I cried. "I am actually abroad . . . for the very first time!" Before I could stop myself, I leapt in the air in a sort of crazy star jump.

"Swanchester does seem a very long way away," beamed Gran.

"Y..." I tried to agree. But my throat was too tight. All I could do was nod. That familiar fizzy feeling was starting to tingle in my toes.

"We've landed half an hour late," said Gran, looking up at the big clock above the luggage carousel. "Anthony will be here any minute now."

POP!

The tingling feeling shot right to the top of my skull and **EXPLODED** like fireworks.

At the mention of Anthony, my last hope of staying calm was gone. I just had time to see Tiffany reach out to grab her big suitcase as it slid past her on the moving belt when...

"Whoa!"

I had shrunk to the size of a luggage label.

In an instant, I was down among people's feet. The wheels of their trolleys THUNDERED past as they pushed towards the spinning carousel.

Tiffany had her back to me and hadn't seen a thing. I don't think Gran had noticed either. She was reaching out to grab my suitcase, which was just behind Tiffany's.

"Yikes!"

I leapt sideways as someone's foot flew towards me like a speeding car.

WHAM!

I jumped out of the way far enough not to be **squashed** flat but the edge of their sandal still caught me.

WHEEEEE.

I was flicked up in the air like a spinning stone.

"Oh no!" I rolled myself into a ball, waiting for the terrible thud as I came back down and hit the hard floor beneath me.

Flump!

Landing on something soft, I opened my eyes and saw that I was clinging to a red leather suitcase.

The suitcase was moving.

I must be on somebody's trolley, I thought. But as I stared down I saw that I was on a moving luggage carousel.

SWOOSH!

A pair of big black rubber curtains closed around me like giant bat wings and the arrivals hall, Gran and Tiff all disappeared from view.

CHAPTER 7

It was dark on the other side of the curtains, in the back part of the luggage carousel. Three men were shouting to one another as they threw suitcases on to the belt.

BOOF!

A big metal trunk landed in front of me.

I was thrown upwards like a coin being flipped into the air.

SPLAT!

I landed back on the belt with my arms and legs spread out like one of those little sticky men you throw at the wall then watch them slide down.

More suitcases crashed on to the belt beside me.

"Yikes!"

I rolled out of the way ... but had to roll back again to the middle of the belt to stop myself from being sucked down over the edge of the plastic flaps and into the cogs of the machine.

Luckily the light was too dim and the men were too busy working to see me. But, as the belt rolled on, I knew any minute now I'd be back in the bright lights of the arrivals hall.

I tried to scramble to my feet.

"Whoa!"

My tiny legs shot out from underneath me and I landed flat on my back like a starfish.

"Whoops!" I giggled. This was fun. Trying to run on the moving belt was like being on one of those exercise machines Mum uses at the gym . . . except there was nothing to hold on to.

SWOOSH!

The black plastic curtains brushed over my head.

I looked up as rows of jostling passengers stared at the carousel, waiting for their luggage to come into view. I had to hide quickly or someone would see me now I was back in the light. I needed to reach one of the cases so I could duck underneath it. Running was hopeless.

The soft rubbery belt felt a bit like the mats we use in gym at school. I flung my legs up into a handstand, flipped over and managed a perfect teeny-tiny handspring towards a moving bag.

"Whee hee!" I cheered. I'd been practising handsprings for weeks. That tiny one was just about the best I'd ever done.

Now I was hidden at last.

I squinted at the black sports bag above me. A little blue and gold Egyptian pharaoh key ring was hanging from the handle. It was exactly the same size as I was. There was a luggage label too.

A. Small was written across it in scruffy, wobbly handwriting a bit like mine. Then there was an address in Sydney, Australia.

Crazy crocodiles! *A. Small* – this was Anthony's bag I was hiding under! I should have known. With a key ring like that, this bag had to belong to my Egypt-crazy cousin. I couldn't wait to show him my little Egyptian mummy key ring – they'd make a great pair.

I saw Gran and Tiff hurrying towards the carousel. Gran was looking around frantically. I knew she must be searching for me. She'd guess that I'd SHRUNK. But that only made things worse for her as she had no idea where I'd gone.

Even Tiffany had taken her earphones out and was looking around as she chewed her gum.

She probably thought I'd just gone to the toilet or something.

"This is the luggage from the Australian flight," said Gran, jogging alongside the belt. "The plane must have landed by now. I do wish I could find Violet."

"She's so rude. She won't even be here to meet Anthony," sighed Tiff.

"I'm sure she's around here somewhere," said Gran, still dashing along beside the belt. "We'll just have to keep an eye out for both of them."

"Gran!" I raised my tiny arm and waved up at her. But it was no use. She was staring anxiously towards the arrivals door looking for Anthony one minute and down at the floor, searching hopelessly for me, the next.

At least if I stay with Anthony's luggage, I won't get lost, I thought.

I slipped under one of the handles, dangling next to the little key ring. The pharaoh's green glass eyes sparkled in the darkness as we disappeared through the black curtains and round to the back of the carousel again.

"Wherever you're going, ANCIENT MAJESTY," I giggled, holding tightly to the tiny Pharaoh's hand, "I'm coming with you." But there was a sudden **rumbling** in my stomach – a **whooshing** feeling like I was running flat out down a hill.

"Uh oh, I know what this means," I whispered.

WHOOSH!

I shot back to full size.

The three luggage workers were staring at

me, their eyes **wide** with surprise, as I rode past them on the carousel. I suppose it's not every day you see a ten-year-old girl sitting cross-legged in among the moving suitcases. Now I was full-size, I was clutching Anthony's sports bag on my lap.

"Good day, mates," I said in what I hoped sounded like an Australian accent. "I've just come to get my things."

"You are not allowed back here," shouted one of the luggage workers.

"Sorry. No worries, mate." I waved as I reached the curtain heading back out to the airport.

"Ouch!" The thick rubber flaps hit me hard in the face.

It wasn't easy getting through now I was full size.

"Oi! Give that case to me," a real, proper-sounding Australian voice shouted as I came out into the light.

"Get off," I yelped, pulling the bag away before I could see who was on the other end.

THUD!

The small, skinny boy who had been tugging at the bag landed on the belt beside me.

"Give me back my stuff!" he yelped.

"*Your* stuff?" I said. "This is my cousin's bag. Unless. . . Oh no. I'm sorry. Anthony? Is that you?"

The skinny boy was about my age. He had sparkly blue eyes, freckles on his nose and short, spiky hair the same chocolatey brown colour

as mine. Now I was looking at him properly, I
recognized him from all the family photos I'd seen.

"Er . . . sorry, Anthony."

I couldn't think of any easy way to explain how
I had ended up hugging his bag. Instead, I held up
my hand and offered him a high five.

"Nice to meet you, Cousin," I grinned.

Anthony folded his arms. "You shouldn't have touched my things," he said.

What was he making such a fuss about? At least he was getting a ride on the carousel.

"Violet?" Tiffany was staring at us, her eyes wide as make-up mirrors, as we passed by. "What are you doing on there?"

"Children, get down." A security guard raced towards us. "No riding on the belt. It is very dangerous."

"Violet ... Anthony ... thank goodness," beamed Gran. "You found each other. Well done."

"What a cool ride, Ant," I whooped as we climbed down from the belt.

But Anthony just stared at the floor.

Why was he being so grumpy? I couldn't help

feeling a little disappointed. This wasn't the crazy, adventure-mad cousin I'd been hoping for. Surely he could see our spin on the carousel had been **BRILLIANT** fun?

CHAPTER 8

Over the next four days, I fell ABSOLUTELY in love with Egypt.

SOLVE IT! had arranged for us to visit all the tourist sites we could manage before it was time to join the archeological dig.

We went to the pyramids first. They were like huge, pointy building bricks a giant baby had left in the middle of the desert. Then we took a train to the famous Valley of the Kings, where we got to see Tutankhamun's SPOOKY mummy with its dry, cracked skin like crinkled leather.

We rode camels and I scampered in among the huge ram-headed sphinxes, all lined up in a row like gigantic London buses.

Everything we saw was **ANCIENT**, **AMAZING** and *AWESOME!*

Thank goodness Gran had found me a jar of pickled walnuts in the hotel bar. They looked like tiny shrivelled-up mummy brains and tasted like slugs in vinegar – but at least I didn't shrink.

The best bit of all was still to come, though.

The part of the trip I was most excited about was travelling up the River Nile in a boat to join our very own archaeological dig.

"Imagine if we uncover a lost tomb," I said, jiggling up and down in the taxi which *SOLVE IT!* had sent to take us to the dock.

I was squashed in the back seat between Anthony and Tiff. "We might even dig up a headless mummy if we're lucky."

"Ew, Violet! You're so gross," said Tiffany, who was trying to wrestle her hair into a pony tail. It had gone WILD AND FRIZZY in the heat.

"It's not very likely we'd actually dig up a mummy, is it?" said Anthony, without even looking up from his smartphone. I glanced over his shoulder. As usual, he was playing his favourite game – some running, jumping, beeping thing called Maze of the Mummy. Every time he slid his fingers across the screen, a mini Egyptian pharaoh swerved through a ruined tomb, gathering scarab beetle jewels as he went.

"You wouldn't care if we *did* find a real mummy," I sighed. "Not unless it earned you a thousand points and took you up to level ten of your stupid game."

PING!

Anthony moved his thumb, sliding back a door to open a virtual tomb, and ignored me.

Typical! I longed for a cousin to play with ... and he turned out to be just as bad as Tiff. The only thing she cares about is make-up and mirrors. With Anthony it's Maze of the Mouldy Mummy! No imagination, either of them.

It's not that I don't like playing computer games ... I'm brilliant at that one where you have to slice a zillion pizzas as quick as you can with a kung fu chop. But not when the real Egypt is all around us. Anthony even played while we were in the tummy-tinglingly creepy tombs at the Valley of the Kings.

"I do think you should put your game away soon, Anthony," said Gran, turning round in the front seat and smiling at both of us. "But don't forget, Violet, it's a very long flight from Australia. I expect Anthony's just tired. All this sightseeing in the last few days must have been exhausting for him."

"I suppose so," I mumbled.

I knew Gran was trying to make peace between us but Anthony was not one little bit like I had hoped he would be. I remembered how desperate I'd been to meet him, especially after his excited emails. He'd sounded like he was about to pop when he said he wanted to be an Egyptologist and discover amazing ancient facts. Now he barely even smiled. It was almost as if a different boy had come along on the trip.

But perhaps Gran was right. Australia was a long way away. He probably was just tired . . . maybe a little homesick too.

"Hey, Ant," I said, tapping his shoulder and trying to think of something nice to say, "wouldn't it be cool if we saw crocodiles on the Nile? They might remind you of home."

"Look what you've done," he snapped, madly tapping the screen. "You made me miss the Tomb of Treasure. That's worth five hundred points. And my name's not Ant; it's Anthony."

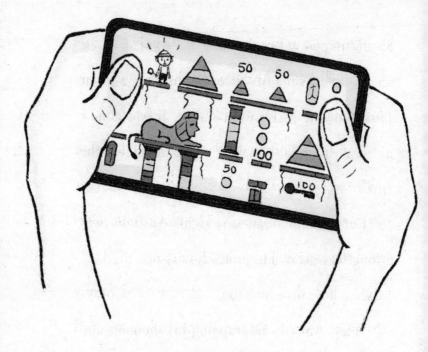

"You signed your emails Ant. . ." I began.

"There are no crocodiles on this part of the Nile anyway," he interrupted, "and, even if there were, why would they remind me of home? I live in Sydney. It's a big city – not the Australian Outback. I don't see crocs driving round in taxis or playing on the swings when I go to the park, you know."

"Fine. I was just trying to be friendly," I said.

"Well, don't." Anthony hunched his shoulders and went back to his stupid game . . . yet again.

I stared out of the window. A truck piled high with watermelons was blocking the street. Our taxi was honking furiously. Three men on scooters were shouting and waving their arms.

A man with a donkey cart plodded calmly through the chaos. I smiled as the donkey twitched its ears and tried to poke its head through the taxi window. Anthony wasn't going to ruin my holiday – no matter how grumpy he wanted to be.

"This is stupid. We're not even moving," groaned Tiff.

Then suddenly the watermelon lorry backed

up, our taxi shot forward – and we could see the River Nile!

"There's your boat," said our taxi driver. "She's called the *Cleopatra*, after Egypt's most beautiful queen."

"That's the perfect name," I cried, peering at the long wooden boat with two big white sails rippling in the breeze.

When the taxi had parked, I FLUNG open the door and scrambled out over Tiffany's knee.

"Those must be the cabins," I said, pointing to a row of little windows just above the water. "I can't believe I'm going to fall asleep tonight floating down the Nile."

I opened my jar of pickled walnuts and popped a whole one in my mouth.

Even Anthony had climbed out of the taxi now. He was standing on tiptoe trying to get better a view of the *Cleopatra*. I spotted a flush of pink in his cheeks.

"Wow!" he whispered.

"Isn't it exciting? We're going to be real explorers," I grinned.

"Archaeologists. . ." Anthony almost smiled. Then a big dark cloud passed over his face as if he had remembered something.

"Are you all right?" I asked, peering sideways at him from under the enormous sunhat I had promised Mum I would wear in the heat.

"I'm fine." Anthony pulled his own cap down over his eyes. "I'm just hot," he snapped. "I'd be a whole lot better if you'd leave me alone and mind your own business for once."

He scrabbled in his bag and pulled out his phone again. I should have guessed. For a moment I had thought he had some deep, mysterious secret he wanted to share … but he was just a grizzly grumpy games nerd who was determined not to have a good time.

Even Tiffany was livelier than him. She hadn't bothered to take any pictures of the amazing ancient sights we had seen on the trip so far, but now she grabbed her phone out of her bag and started snapping pictures of the fancy-looking boat.

"You can show off to all your friends your social-face-thingy page," smiled Gran.

"Monique is going to be *so* jealous," beamed

Tiff, actually jumping up and down as she spotted a row of gold-fringed sun loungers lined up on the deck. "As soon as the boat sails, I am not going to move from there," she said.

"Isn't it glamorous?" whistled Gran, grabbing Tiffany's hand. The three of us jumped up and down together. "It's like something from a film."

I looked at the smooth wooden boat, her tall masts creaking in the wind. Gran was right. The *Cleopatra* was the poshest, most perfect-looking boat I had ever seen.

I ≡ **dashed** forward and ran up the sloping gangplank. "You can lie on a sun lounger if you like, Tiff," I called, "but I'm all set for a real Egyptian adventure."

CHAPTER 9

"Welcome aboard the *Cleopatra*. My name is Musa."

A young Egyptian man, not much older than Tiffany, stepped away from a small group of smartly dressed passengers, who all looked like fancy millionaires or movie stars.

"You must be our four lucky prize winners," he smiled. "I'll be your guide for our journey along the Nile and also when we reach the site of the archaeological dig where you will help us discover lost treasures buried in the sand."

"Hi..." I stopped and looked down as

something purred and wound itself around my ankles.

"Meet Ozymandias, the ship's cat," chuckled Musa, as Tiffany snapped a picture.

"He's named after a famous poem about Egypt. But it's a very big name for a little puss, so we just call him Ozzy."

As if he knew we were talking about him, Ozzy stuck his nose in the air and strutted up and down the sunny deck like a supermodel in a fashion show. Even the smartly dressed passengers glanced over at him.

"I think he wants us all to admire him," laughed Gran.

"He's beautiful," I said as Ozzy wound himself around my ankles again. He didn't look anything like the scruffy old moggies I help to look after at the PAW THINGS PET RESCUE centre in Swanchester. He was more like a miniature panther with his silver-grey fur, sharp pointy ears and bright emerald-green eyes.

"He's just like the statues of the ancient cats we saw at the British Museum," said Gran.

"He gives me the creeps a bit," shuddered Tiff.

"Only because he is even more vain than you are," I laughed as Ozzy arched his back so that I could pat him more easily. "I think he's gorgeous."

"**MAAAW**," Ozzy gave a high-pitched miaow.

"Sounds more like a baby crying than a cat," frowned Anthony, looking up from his game.

"Poor little guy. Perhaps he's hungry," said a plump old lady sitting at a table nearby. She had a strong American accent. "Here you go, puss," she cooed, pouring a saucer of milk from a silver tea set and sliding it across the deck towards Ozzy. She looked up and smiled at me. "Howdy. My name's Miss June Calendar and this is my sister, Miss July."

Another round, smiley little old lady raised her
tea cup and waved at us. Tiffany was still snapping
away with her camera.

"We're just crazy about cats," said Miss June.

"Me too. I work at a pet rescue centre in my
spare time," I explained.

I was about to tell them how Nisha and I are always playing with the kittens, when the *Cleopatra* suddenly shuddered forward.

"We're moving," I cried.

I looked up and saw that the wind had filled the huge white sails.

"Hooray!" I cheered, throwing my spotty sunhat high in the air. "We're off to the archaeological site to dig in the ruins."

I really did feel like a proper pharaoh-finding explorer as we left the city and the crowds of tourists far behind. I lay on the deck, flat on my tummy, staring down at the water.

"We're going on a dig. We're going on a dig," I whispered in time to the waves as they splashed against the side of the boat.

Gran had gone down to her cabin for an afternoon nap. Anthony was dozing on a cushion beside me. Tiffany, of course, was lying like a lizard on one of the sun loungers.

Even Ozzy was ready for a snooze. He'd been sharing smoked salmon nibbles at the bar with a millionaire Italian businessman named Signor Sipperetto. But once the fish was all gone, he had padded over to the side of the boat and curled himself up on the open pages of my *Bumper Book of Ancient Egypt*.

Signor Sipperetto waved at me.

I'd spent most of the morning meeting people and making friends. There were the old, cat-loving Calendar sisters, of course. And Signora Sipperetto, the millionaire's wife. She was the only person who seemed to have any energy left in the boiling hot sun. She was sprinting up and down the deck, dressed in a bright pink tracksuit, timing herself on a stop watch.

The Sipperettos had the huge luxury cabin next door to the tiny one which Tiff and I shared. (I had got the top bunk, of course. Yippee!)

The big posh cabin opposite us belonged a French couple who were in Egypt on honeymoon. Everywhere they went they were always holding hands and kissing.

Yuck! I thought, blushing red as a tomato as I spotted them standing at the front of the boat, staring into each other's eyes like something from one of the romantic, slushy

-mushy movies

Tiffany always

makes us watch

when it's her turn to

choose a DVD.

The only person I hadn't met yet was in the little cabin next to Anthony and Gran.

I glanced over at Anthony to ask if he'd seen anyone. But his baseball cap was pulled down over his eyes, so I guessed he was still asleep.

"Never mind," I whispered to Ozzy. "I want to find out more about ANCIENT EGYPT anyway. Then I'll know what to look out for when we reach the dig. . . If only you'd move over a little!"

I lifted Ozzy's paw and began to read all about *shabti*. There was a brilliant picture of them, little figures just like the ones Gran and I had seen at the British Museum.

"Enjoying your book?" said a voice above me. A wide shadow fell across the page.

I looked up to see a big fat man with pink

cheeks and little round glasses.

"Hello," I smiled.

This must be the last passenger.

"Good gracious, it's you!" The man, who had the loudest, poshest English voice I had ever heard, let out a gasp of surprise. Then he shook himself as if he'd seen a ghost. "Forgive me. I thought for a moment we had met someplace . . . somewhere . . . before. But we haven't. . . ."

"No," I agreed, "I don't think so."

"Definitely not." He held out his hand. "My name's Professor Gus. Delighted to meet you, my dear. I'm an Egyptologist."

"Wow!" I grinned, shaking his hand. "You must have the best job in the whole wide world. I wish my cousin was awake."

Finding out we had a real Egyptologist on the
boat might actually make Anthony excited about
the trip at long last.

"I bet you know zillions of amazing things
about Ancient Egypt," I said. "I've only done a
school project but I'd love to know more."

"Well, you've come to the right person. I'm
a world-famous expert," boomed the professor,

rocking back on his heels and looking very pleased with himself. He seemed to have recovered from whatever had surprised him a few moments earlier. "Shall I tell you something really, really gory about Ancient Egypt?" he asked.

"Yes, please – the gorier the better," I grinned, leaning forward and hoping the professor was about to reveal some hideous, horrible secret he had discovered from a long-lost hieroglyph.

"The mummy-makers used to remove people's brains," he whispered.

"...That *is* horrible," I said, trying my best to sound surprised. But I had learnt all about it for my school project, of course.

"You'll never ever guess how they did it," said the professor.

"They poked a hook up the dead person's nose and pulled the brains out through their nostrils," I said, before I could stop myself.

"Well, I see you have no need for me," huffed the professor, turning away.

"Sorry..." I blushed, scrambling to my feet. "I didn't mean to ... to interrupt you. It's just I wrote a diary of a mummy-maker. And I read all about it in here too." I pointed to where Ozzy was still curled up fast asleep on my *Bumper Book of Ancient Egypt*. There was a really gory drawing of how mummification worked.

"Of course. You have *that* book. How silly of me." The professor stuck out his bottom lip.

"It really is a BRILLIANT, eyeball-popping, HORRIBLE, TOTALLY gruesome fact,"

I said. I hadn't meant to offend the professor. After all, he must have studied the Ancient Egyptians for years and years. I was just talking about something I'd read in a children's book.

"I'll have you know, I'm one of the five most famous Egyptologists in the world," he boomed.

"That's strange," said a voice beside me.

It was Anthony. I spun round and saw that he was wide awake. His nap obviously hadn't improved his mood. Instead of looking pleased to meet the professor he was frowning at him.

"If you're such an expert on Egypt, what are you doing on a tourist boat like this?" he asked.

"Anthony," I hissed. What was he thinking of, talking to the famous Egyptologist like that?

"Ignore my cousin, Professor," I apologized. "He fell asleep so he hasn't played on his electronic game for at least twenty minutes. It makes him grumpy, I'm afraid."

But Professor Gus just smiled and shook his head. "Young man," he said, pointing up the Nile in the direction we were sailing. "I have come to join your archaeological quest. I am as eager as you are to see what we will discover at the Temple of the Cats."

"The Temple of the Cats?" I gasped. A shiver ran down my spine. The name sounded so exciting and mysterious. "Is that the place where we're going to dig?"

"Didn't you know, my dear?" The professor bent down and scooped up Ozzy as if he were an ancient treasure lying in the sand. "Our little group is set to explore a long-lost burial site dedicated to the Egyptian worship of cats."

"MAAAW," Ozzy yowled and leapt out of the professor's arms.

CHAPTER 10

Dinner that night was delicious.

We ate sticky honey chicken with rice and giant slices of watermelon, all sitting round a long table up on deck.

It was super fancy – with gold cutlery and little bowls of water, which I thought we were meant to drink.

"Violet," hissed Gran, nudging me in the ribs. "You're only supposed to wash your fingers in those."

"Whoops!" I said, but nobody seemed to have noticed.

I glanced around, sneaking another good look at everyone now we were all in the same place.

"It's a bit like one of those whodunit mysteries, isn't it?" whispered Gran from behind her napkin. I knew she fancied herself as Miss Marple, a little-old-lady detective she often watches on the telly. "Everyone's gathered together," she said, winking mysteriously. "And we have to guess who the baddy is."

"Except nobody's done anything wrong . . . as far as we know," I giggled.

The only person who even looked slightly guilty was Signor Sipperetto – and that was only because he was having an extra-big second helping of sticky chicken. Professor Gus was sitting next to him, busily explaining something to the Calendar sisters. He was waving his arms in the air. The two old ladies were leaning forward, their heads bent close together, looking worried.

"Oh dear! I hope he's not telling them how the Ancient Egyptians used to sacrifice cats," I murmured to Gran, remembering the horrible things we'd read about at the British Museum.

"I suppose we'll find out more about that sort of thing at the temple," said Gran.

"SPOOKY!" I shuddered, nearly knocking over Tiffany's glass. She didn't even notice. She was too busy staring at the young French honeymooners, Lola and Louis L'Amour. She hadn't taken her eyes off them all through dinner and had even managed a couple of sneaky photos on her phone.

"Don't they make a beautiful couple?" Tiff sighed. "Louis is as handsome as a movie star. And I've seen a picture of Lola in a magazine. She's some sort of model, I think. Just look at her little black dress. It is *so* classic."

"Really?" I said. The dress just looked short and black to me. Although, I had to admit, everyone did seem to be wearing their fanciest clothes. The men had bow ties and most of the women wore glittery diamonds, which twinkled in the lantern light like Christmas decorations. Even Gran had put on a sparkly, rainbow-coloured shirt and Tiffany had chosen her teeniest tiniest mini skirt (which she thinks is really smart – although Dad says it's so short it looks like she's forgotten to get dressed at all!).

For one supersonic second, I *almost* wished I'd brought the frilly pink party dress Mum had tried to make me pack. *Almost*... But my favourite purple spotty trousers were far more comfortable and a zillion times more cool!

"Yuck!" I gulped, nudging Tiffany in the ribs as Lola and Louis actually kissed right there at the table!

"Honestly, Violet, you're so immature," sniffed Tiff, sipping her orange juice with her little finger raised. "I think it's romantic."

I glanced over at Anthony. Surely he'd agree all this lovey-dovey stuff was enough to put you off your dinner. But he'd hardly said a word all evening. He was sitting opposite me, staring down at his lap.

"Hopeless!" I sighed. He must be playing **Maze of the Mummy** under the tablecloth. He probably hadn't even noticed that the sky had turned black and there was a huge moon above us now.

But just as I was about to flick a watermelon pip at him, he suddenly looked up.

"Wouldn't it be incredible if we really did find a cat mummy at the temple?" he said, as if he had been listening to my conversation with Gran five minutes ago.

"It would be completely and utterly tomb-tremblingly amazing, Ant," I agreed.

For the first time on the whole trip, he had a smile as big as a crocodile on his face. He didn't even correct me for not calling him Anthony.

"Imagine if we discovered something really

rare or precious," he grinned. For a moment he seemed like the boy who had sent me all those emails – the one who was totally mummy-mad and Ancient Egypt-crazy. "When Tutankhamun was a young pharaoh, he would have sailed along the Nile, looking at the stars, just like we are now," he said. I could hear the excitement rising in his voice.

"I know." I nodded and my heart began to pound too as we both stared up at the zillions of twinkling dots above our heads. I dug in my pocket and popped an emergency pickled walnut into my mouth.

"I can't believe we're actually here," I gulped, "on our way to the dig. . ." But as I glanced across the table, I saw that Anthony's chair was empty.

"Ant. . .?" I called. "Anthony. . .? Where've you gone?"

"I expect he's slipped down to the cabin," said Gran, who was chattering like the best of friends with Miss June and Miss July.

"Typical!" I groaned, staring at Anthony's empty chair. Just when I thought he was going to be more fun! He must have sloped off to play mind-numbing Maze of the Mummy as usual.

It's strange though, I thought, as I helped myself to the big juicy slice of watermelon Anthony had left on his plate. *He was here* literally *one second ago. . .*

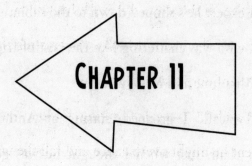

CHAPTER 11

This time tomorrow we'll arrive at the dig, I thought as I bounded out on deck early next morning, expecting to be the first person awake.

I was wrong.

The Calendar sisters were already up. They were tiptoeing between the sun loungers, calling to Ozzy.

"Here, puss," they cooed, holding out a tin of sardines. They were obviously desperate to spoil him with a delicious breakfast.

But Ozzy was being far too snooty. He was

balancing on the ship's rail, with his tail curled in the air, as if he had much more interesting things to do than jump down and eat fish.

"Careful," I cried, thinking for one terrible moment he might overbalance and fall the wrong way – into the Nile.

But Ozzy was too clever for that. He leapt down in one bound and curled himself around my ankles.

"Good morning, Violet, dear," cried the old ladies, turning as they saw me. Miss June was wearing an orange stripy shirt and Miss July, who was just as round as her sister, was wearing a bright flowery skirt. Standing side by side, the two smiling old ladies reminded me of a pair of comfy old arm chairs.

"Did you sleep well?" asked Miss July.

"Brilliantly," I said. The *Cleopatra* had rocked me to sleep like a baby in a cradle. Poor Tiff hadn't been so lucky – the rocking didn't agree with her and she had felt horribly seasick (or riversick to be precise). I'd left her moaning and groaning in our cabin with her face the same green colour as one of Mum's most disgusting spinach bakes.

"I bet you're looking forward to the dig at the Temple of the Cats," said Miss June, sitting herself down at one of the little wicker tables.

"I can't wait," I smiled, flopping down in the chair beside her and swinging my legs with excitement.

"I'm desperate to see the cute kitties myself," said Miss June.

"Adorable pussycats," agreed Miss July.

"Er…" I thought the two cat-loving old ladies would be a little upset to find they were heading to a temple where they might discover a two-thousand-year-old mummified moggy all wrapped up in bandages. Not exactly what I'd call *cute* or *adorable*…

"We'll have to bring plenty of milk," said Miss June.

"And some lovely fishy treats too," smiled Miss July, pointing to the tin of sardines, which Ozzy was finally eating.

"Miss June … Miss July," I said carefully. "You do know the cats at the temple are dead, don't you? I mean *very dead*. Thousands of years dead."

"Gracious me, yes," laughed Miss June.

"We're not talking about *ancient* cats," said

Miss July. "We shan't be digging for relics with the rest of you. We'll be far too busy with the poor modern kitties, I'm afraid."

"What do you mean?" I asked.

"Wherever there are ancient ruins to shelter in from the heat, there are always stray cats who need feeding," said Miss June.

"We run an organization called Cat Lovers of the Ancient World. CLAW for short," explained Miss July.

"We've travelled the world helping to rescue kitties. First Greece, then the Colosseum in Rome – it's famous for its stray cats – and now here in Egypt," said Miss June. "It's our mission at CLAW to help save all the poor pussycats we can."

"Like an animal charity?" I asked. I told the old ladies how Uncle Max had got our dog Chip from the **PAW THINGS PET RESCUE** Centre.

"Then you understand how important our work is," said Miss July. "We were very poor when we were growing up back home in the United States. There were twelve of us Calendar children, eleven girls and one boy..."

"We were all named after a different month of the year," interrupted Miss June. "Even our dear brother, August."

"But no matter how poor we were, we always had a cat," went on Miss July. "To help catch the mice and the rats."

While we'd been talking, Ozzy had finished his sardines. He'd jumped on to Miss June's lap and was cleaning his whiskers.

"CLAW is our way of saying thank you," Miss June said, SNEEZING into a handkerchief as tears rolled down her cheeks. She was WHEEZING loudly.

"Those cats are lucky to have you," I said.

To look at the two little old ladies, you'd think a game of bingo would be an adventure for them. Instead, they travelled the world, helping strays in ancient ruins... No wonder they'd got on so well with Gran at dinner – they were just about as crazy as she was.

"We do so love the poor little kitty-cats," sniffed Miss June, dabbing her red eyes. "But I'm afraid this handsome fellow is hurting my bad knee. Run along now. Shoo!" She pushed Ozzy firmly off her lap.

Hiss! Ozzy arched his back and spat at her.

"Don't be so cross," I scolded him. Miss June's poor old knees must be really sore for her to push him off her like that.

"Gorgeous creatures, but moody," said Miss July, shaking her head as Ozzy strutted away.

"If only we didn't need to raise so much money to care for them," SNEEZED Miss June, blowing her nose.

"So very much money," agreed Miss July. "Milk and fish and vets' bills. It never ends."

"Mum gave me some spending money for the trip," I said. "I was saving it to buy the perfect souvenir. It's not much but you can have that."

"Darling child." Miss June heaved herself out

of her chair and grabbed hold of my hands. "You are an angel."

"A gem," agreed Miss July. I blushed pink as bubble gum. "Even a little pocket money can help CLAW save an abandoned cat. Though we need so very much more than that. . ."

As Miss July gathered me into a hug, I spotted Anthony coming up the stairs from his cabin. He raised his eyebrows and sighed loudly.

There's no need to be rude, I thought, scowling

at him. Just because the Calendar sisters were old

and . . . well, a little enthusiastic. Here they were

doing their very best to help the poor abandoned

cats of the world.

"Where did you disappear to last night?" I asked him as we went to the side of the boat and looked down at the river. "One minute you were staring at the stars, the next you were gone."

"I wanted to reach level ten on **Maze of the Mummy**," shrugged Anthony. "I could see you were going to keep talking. I went down to my cabin to play in peace."

"That is SO unfair. You were talking just as much as I was," I cried. "All about Tutankhamun and what we might find on the dig…" I was so furious I had a good mind to push Anthony into the Nile and hope a stray crocodile would swim along and GOBBLE him up.

Luckily for him, Musa, our guide, appeared from the kitchen. *That's strange,* I thought. He was waving Anthony's phone in the air.

"I found this under the table when I cleared up after dinner," Musa called.

"Hold on a mini moment. You told me you were playing **Maze of the Mummy** in your cabin," I said, turning to Anthony, who was shuffling from one foot to the other like a fidgeting flea. "But you can't have been. You didn't even have your phone."

"Just keep your freckly nose out of my business, will you?" Anthony hissed. His hands were shaking as he grabbed his phone and stormed away.

"Wait," I called. "What's going on?"

But Anthony had already run back downstairs.

CHAPTER 12

When Gran came up for breakfast, the Calendar sisters told her all about their work for CLAW too.

I wasn't really listening any more. I was too busy wondering what Anthony was up to. I asked Gran if she had seen him since he stormed away.

"He's in our cabin, playing that silly computer game again," she sighed. "I hate to be a strict grandma, but I'll have to take it from him if this goes on. He's missing half the holiday, staring at that screen."

"Exactly," I said, triumphantly.

But then a thought struck me. Perhaps that wasn't what Anthony was doing in his cabin at all. He had certainly lied to me about having his phone last night.

"Any idea where Tiffany's got to?" said Gran, interrupting my thoughts.

"In bed," I said. "She's as green as a croc. I don't think she likes being on a boat much."

"I'm sorry your sister is not feeling well," said Musa, overhearing us as he poured Gran a coffee. "We're going to visit a local market this morning. They have beautiful jewellery and cloth for sale..."

"Perfect! Nothing cheers Tiff up more than a bit of shopping," I smiled.

"We can see if they have some supplies for the cats," said Miss June. "After all, we arrive at the temple tomorrow."

"Things in the market might be cheap," agreed Miss July. "Money is always such a worry for us. Every penny counts towards helping the cats."

"Hmm," Gran nodded. I wondered if she was thinking the same thing as me. Although we'd won our tickets as a prize, I knew that a cruise on a luxury boat like the *Cleopatra* was super-duper expensive.

"Of course, we do splash out a bit on travel," said Miss June shyly, as if reading my mind. "At our age the little comforts make such a difference and a good rest means we have plenty of energy to help the cats when we arrive."

"Quite right," said Gran. "Just because we're not millionaires in real life, doesn't mean we can't pretend a little when we're on holiday."

"Flying piggy banks, you're a genius, Gran," I cried.

What she said had given me a brilliant idea. We might not be real millionaires ourselves but everyone else on this boat seemed to be as rich as the ancient pharaohs.

I looked across at the sun loungers where Signor Sipperetto was tickling Ozzy behind the ears and already sipping his first morning glass of champagne. Signora Sipperetto was jogging up and down the deck, shouting at someone on her sparkly, jewel-studded mobile phone. Her personal trainer, I guessed.

Lola and Louis L'Amour were leaning on a rail nearby. Louis's big gold watch caught the light. It shone like Ra the Egyptian sun god. Lola had yet another new outfit on and a diamond ring the size of one of Ozzy's paws.

"Listen," I whispered to Gran and the Calendar sisters. "Everyone else on this boat really *is* a millionaire – except perhaps Professor Gus. We should ask them all to donate some money to CLAW. To help the cats."

"You can't just ask people for money, Violet," said Gran. "It's rude."

"It doesn't work quite like that, I'm afraid," agreed Miss July.

"But what if we had had a fundraiser?" I said. "Like we did at school when we needed new equipment for our gym club."

"Now that *is* an idea," said Miss June.

"We raised money by letting everyone wear their own clothes instead of school uniform for a day," I explained. "Whoever wanted to take part had to pay."

"I don't see how that would work on the boat," said Miss July. "We're all wearing our own clothes already. . ."

"We could have a fancy dress party for the passengers," I said. "On our last night – to celebrate the end of the holiday. Anyone who wants to wear a costume has to make a donation to CLAW. Our family will probably only be able to pay a pound or two each . . . but some of the other passengers might give a lot more. Especially when they know what a good cause it is."

"I think it's a terrific plan," said Miss June.

"Signor Sipperetto really likes cats, so that is a good start," I said as I watched him tickle Ozzy under the chin.

"Lola L'Amour wept buckets when I told her about the poor strays," said Miss July.

"It's decided then." I clapped my hands.

"We'll have to ask Musa, but I am sure he'll agree. He's such a softie about Ozzy," said Gran.

"It's going to be totally pharaoh-tastic!" I grinned. "We can look for bits and pieces for our costumes at the market."

"It's a wonderful idea, Violet. Thank you from all the poor kitties of the world," beamed Miss June.

CHAPTER 13

Musa agreed at once that the party could go ahead.

"I think I'll dress up as a camel," laughed Gran as we made our way up the hot dusty path towards the little town where the market was. "I've got a big yellow T-shirt and some baggy gold trousers. All I'll need to do is stuff a pillow up my back to make a hump."

"I'm going to be Cleopatra," said Tiffany, who was looking a little less green now she was off the moving boat. "She was totally gorgeous. I've seen pictures of what she was supposed to look like . . . I think I have her nose."

"If you have her nose, you better give it back," I giggled, but Gran poked me in the ribs.

"How about you, Anthony?" she asked. "Who are you going to be?"

"Nobody," he growled, staring down at his stupid game. He tripped on the path. "I don't want to dress up. Why can't everyone leave me alone?"

"That's it. I have had enough of this," said Gran. "Give me that phone right now."

I've only ever seen Gran get really cross about twice in my life – but now she looked like an angry bull about to charge.

"But. . ." stammered Anthony as she snatched the phone away from him.

"No buts," said Gran firmly. "I'll hold on to this until we get back from the market." She dropped the phone into her handbag. "You're never going to enjoy this trip until you look around and take notice of what's going on," she said, more kindly.

"Take my phone if you want but it is *not* a good idea," muttered Anthony, scowling at us.

"Wow!" I said, taking off my hat to fan my face as the sun beat down. "This place is amazing." Surely even Anthony could see how incredible it was?

Sacks of spice as green and red and orange as traffic lights were spread out along the pavement. An old man with no teeth dug his hand into a basket like the one we have for dirty laundry at home. He pulled out a writhing snake and wound it round his neck.

"This is a LOT more fun than shopping in Swanchester," I whooped as a crowd of jostling boys with gold necklaces to sell shouted prices at us and pushed us on through the narrow streets.

I grabbed at my hat as it was nearly knocked off my head and felt my fingers tingling with excitement.

"Yikes. Not now!" I gulped. I quickly dug into my pocket . . . but I had left my emergency pickled walnuts on the boat.

"Gran," I called. But my voice was lost in the noise of the market.

I flung my arm out, desperate to catch hold of her sleeve. But a man selling sugared dates bustled her towards his stall.

A girl with bunches of peacock feathers grabbed Tiff. I had no idea where Anthony had gone.

"Come back, Gran," I called helplessly. If I **shr**ank in this crowd, I'd be trampled as **FLAT** as a squished raisin.

I pushed forward, trying to make it to the pavement. But I tripped and. . .

WHOOSH!

I SHRANK to the size of a crocodile's tooth.

"AAAAAAA-CHOOO." A giant sneeze shot through my tiny body. I had landed in a sack full of black spice. "Peppercorns!" They looked like cannonballs beside my mini feet. "Aaaaaaaa-choooooooooooo!" I sneezed again.

The force of the blast as it shot through my

pin-sized nostrils was supersonic. It blew me up into the air like a EXPLODING FIREWORK.

I turned a somersault above the sack of pepper, shot forward and landed in a barrel of short brown twigs, each one about as long as I was.

"Ouch." One of them dug into my back. "Cinnamon sticks."

I smiled as a scent of Christmas filled my nostrils. I love the smell of cinnamon. Gran sometimes puts ground sprinkles on toast for me with sugar. It was a whole lot better than the peppercorns. At least I wasn't going to blow myself up from sneezing.

The twigs made pretty good camouflage too. I ducked down inside the barrel, hiding myself like a stick insect in a mesh of tiny branches.

My nose was still tickling from the pepper though.

I dug in my shorts pocket, hoping to find a mini tissue. It would be the smaller than a bumble bee's wing by now. Everything I'm wearing and anything in my pockets always shrinks when I do. But, of course, I didn't have a tissue with me. Mum's always going on at me about sniffing but I never remember to carry tissues, not even on a cold, rainy Swanchester winter day. So I certainly didn't have one here in the sweltering sunshine of Egypt.

"A-choo!"

As I sneezed, I caught a flash of movement out the corner of my eye. Was there a mouse in this barrel with me? Once I ended up in a litter bin with a rat when I shrank at a theme park. It was a giant one – a Ty-RAT-osaurus rex. Don't get me wrong, I like mice, they're cute. I LOVE my hamster, Hannibal. But I am not too keen on rats – especially when I'm just the right size to be mistaken for a chunk of nibbly cheese.

With the little hairs standing up on the back of my neck, I peered between the sticks of cinnamon.

There was nothing there.

Perhaps I was imagining things.

But I had a definite, creepy feeling I was being watched.

I peered upwards to see if someone was looking down into the barrel.

There was nobody.

"Awk." I heard a small, strange, gulping sound behind me. Like a whimper of surprise. I knew hadn't imagined it this time. I was being watched for sure.

"Who's there?" I whispered. My legs were trembling and my heart was fluttering like a cage of swirling butterflies. Very slowly, I turned my head and peered among the sticks of spice.

"You?" I gasped.

I was staring into a pair of small bright-blue eyes, each the size of a grain of rice.

"Anthony?" I spluttered. "You're ... you're as tiny as I am."

My teeny-weeny cousin was dangling by one arm from a cinnamon stick, swaying like a Christmas decoration.

"I don't believe it. . ." I whispered, "you're a shrinker too."

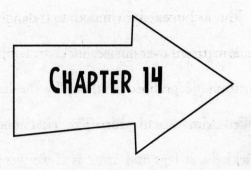

CHAPTER 14

I was so surprised to see Anthony, I opened and closed my mouth like a baby bird in the nest of cinnamon sticks.

I'd always thought I was the only person in the whole world, other than Gran, who'd ever shrunk. Now here was Cousin Anthony, just as small as I was.

There were a zillion questions I wanted to ask him. How long had he been shrinking for? How long did he usually stay tiny? What was his best shrinking adventure ever?

But as I opened my mouth to try and speak, a shadow passed over our heads.

"Quick!" I grabbed Anthony by the hand and pulled him downwards. The cinnamon sticks prickled our legs and arms as if we were falling through the branches of a scratchy, scrapey tree.

The stall holder dug deep into the barrel, his scoop like a giant digger above our heads.

"There you are, madam, that should be plenty," he said, filling a paper bag up to the top.

"Give me more," said an American voice. "Hurry."

The stall holder filled another bag to the brim. The scoop missed my head by a millimetre.

Anthony and I slithered deeper down into the barrel.

"And some nutmeg too. Be quick."

There was a second American voice now and I realized they both sounded familiar.

"Look," I mouthed, tugging Anthony's sleeve. We ducked under a thick stick of cinnamon. "It's the Calendar sisters."

Even buried in the barrel I could see the bright patterns on their clothes.

What did they want so many spices for? As far as I know cats don't like cinnamon and nutmeg in their food.

"Come on." Anthony pointed upwards as their shadows moved away. "Let's get out of here before it's too late."

He was right. One more scoop of spice and we might be sold to another passer-by.

I followed him as he SPRANG from one cinnamon stick to the next, climbing them as if they were the rungs of a ladder. He leapt out of the barrel, ran around the rim of the sack of peppercorns, slid down the seam of the bag, JUMPED – one, two, three – across the bars of a drain cover and SKIDDED to a stop inside the scooped-out skin of an old watermelon, which had rolled under a stall.

"Wow! Where did you learn to move like that?" I gasped, ducking into the melon shell beside him.

I had never even seen Anthony run when he was full-grown. Now he was tiny, he was like a mini action hero.

"Maze of the Mummy," he shrugged. "You don't play computer games as much as I do without learning how to jump around a bit. Touch the floor and POW!" He made a noise like an exploding bomb. "Game over!"

"That's incredible," I said. I'm pretty fit. I'm in the gym club at school and I spend loads of time in the adventure playground in King's Park near our house ... but Anthony was like a tiny runaway ninja.

"Whenever I'm small I just imagine I'm inside a game," he said.

"I reckon you must be on level one zillion and ten," I cheered, holding out my tiny hand to give him a high five. If I'd just planned a route like Anthony's, I'd be grinning from ear to ear. I was smiling now, even though all I'd done was follow his lead. But Anthony's mouth was all pinched up and cross, as if he'd just swallowed a teaspoon of super-yucky cough medicine.

"What's wrong, Ant?" I asked.

"For the last time, my name is not Ant. It is Anthony." He kicked the spongy wall of the empty watermelon, sending a spurt of pink juice splurging past my knees. "Ants are small and stupid. They get squashed by people's shoes."

I was about to tell him that ants are actually pretty clever – like on this nature programme I saw once where they built a moving bridge out of their own bodies. But, suddenly, I understood what was going on.

"Oh, I get it," I said. "You don't like shrinking, do you? You don't like being small."

"Of course I don't." Anthony kicked the watermelon again. High above us, I could hear the sounds of the market going on but down here it was like we were in our own secret cave. "Shrinking is stupid ... and dangerous." His tiny hands were trembling and his face was as white as salt. "Don't tell me you actually like it?"

"I love shrinking," I said. "It is super-scary sometimes. But I always have the most amazing adventures. Once I caught a thief red-handed. Another time, I rode on a real live lion. And look at us now. Here we are in the middle of an Egyptian market and we're smaller than two teaspoons. Anywhere we want to go, anything we want to explore, and we can do it. Nobody will even know we're here."

"Yeah. If we're not squashed like a couple of slugs under someone's shoe," sighed Anthony.

"I do try and stop myself shrinking at the wrong time," I said. "I've been chewing pickled walnuts for days."

"That's why you were eating those disgusting things," said Anthony. "I just thought you liked the taste of vinegar."

"I hate vinegar," I said. "But I shrink when I'm overexcited and eating yucky food stops it sometimes. Is it the same with you?"

"Sort of." Anthony nodded. "I shrank for the very first time when I heard we were coming on this trip. It happened again every time you sent an email talking about all the cool things we were going to do."

"So that's why you stopped replying to me?" I said.

"Yes. I didn't tell anyone," Anthony sighed. "Not even my mum and dad. But it kept happening when I was packing my suitcase and thinking about going on the plane. That's when I knew I had to find a way to take my mind of all the amazing sights I was going to see on this holiday. I've wanted to come to Egypt my whole life. But instead of looking around, I've spent my entire time staring at a screen playing Maze of the Mummy. If I'm concentrating on that stupid game – scoring as many points as I can – I don't seem to shrink."

Anthony's voice was cracking. I saw a tiny tear glisten on his eyelash and realized how upset he was. But I didn't say anything. I never cry . . . well, hardly ever. And I hate it if people see me when I do.

"Listen, you can enjoy the trip from now on," I said. "It's going to be brilliant. We can help each other. I'll even share my pickled walnuts if you like."

"No." Anthony shook his head. "I took my eyes off the screen for one minute at dinner last night. Just to look up at the stars.

Next thing I knew I was stuck under the heel of Lola L'Amour's shoe."

"So that's what happened to you? You shrank," I said, remembering how Anthony had been sitting across the table from me one minute and then had disappeared the next. "I can't believe I never guessed. After all, we have the same grandma." I already knew Gran had passed her shrinking down to me. But Tiffany had never shrunk as far as I knew.

"And that's why Musa found your phone under the table," I said. "You fibbed about going back to your cabin to play Maze of the Mummy."

"I was scampering between people's feet, trying not to be kicked into the River Nile." Anthony shuddered.

"We'll have fun together from now on," I said. "I promise. We can tell Gran the truth and she'll help. Come to think of it, she'll be worrying where we are. We better sneak out of here and find her. Let's go. We can explore the market along the way."

Anthony didn't move. "I don't want to explore. I don't want to have fun. This isn't some stupid game," he said. "Don't you get it, Violet? I've seen bugs in Australia bigger than you and me. Look at us. We're freaks."

"Freaks?" The word was so horrible, it was as if Anthony had **slapped** me in the face.

"I just want to be normal," he said. "And I want you to leave me alone."

He darted out of the watermelon and began to run.

"Wait, Ant," I cried.

"Get lost, Violet," he hissed. "Just stay away."

CHAPTER 15

I was hopping through the market like a grasshopper, searching desperately for Ant, when...

"YIKES!"

I shot back to **full size** right behind the back legs of a camel.

"Careful, she kicks," cried the owner, who hadn't seen me growing tall. But the camel gave me a very strange look, as if to say, "How in the name of hairy humps did you do that?"

"Sorry!" I cried, speeding on through the market to look for Gran and Tiff. I kept my eyes open for Anthony too, but I knew there was probably no chance of spotting him if he was still tiny – especially if he didn't want to be found.

"Violet, there you are." Gran dashed out from behind a hanging carpet and gathered me into a hug. "I've been looking everywhere. I was so worried about you in this crowd," she cried. She must have guessed that I'd shrunk.

Tiffany rolled her eyes, which made her look a lot like the camel. "You shouldn't get in such a panic, Gran," she sighed. "Violet's always getting lost. I bet she was still looking at that horrible snake in the basket."

"Something like that," I said.

"We saw the owner feed it a dead mouse," shuddered Tiffany. "It swallowed it whole. . ."

"At least it won't be hungry for a while," I said, glancing over Gran's shoulder at the crowded market. The last I'd seen him, Anthony had been running back in the direction of the snake. If he was still tiddly he'd make a perfect cobra-sized snack.

Gran stopped hugging me at last. "Have you seen your cousin anywhere?" she asked. "He disappeared almost the same time you did. I think he's sulking because I took away his phone."

"Anthony has a little problem, Gran," I said. "Just a small thing. A tiny bit of bother. . ."

"Gracious me." Gran's hand flew up to her mouth. "You mean . . . like you. . .?"

I nodded.

"I never guessed," said Gran.

"What *are* you talking about?" said Tiffany. "And why are you both staring at the ground. If you're looking for Anthony he's not going to be down there, is he?"

"No." Gran and I both laughed nervously and looked up for a moment. I have always been amazed that Tiff has never guessed about my shrinking. But now I had spent all this time with Anthony and never suspected a thing either, it started to make more sense. I remembered what Gran had said, all those weeks ago when we were searching for the last answer in the wordsearch puzzle: *People don't see what is right under their own noses*. It turns out she was right.

"Anthony's over there anyway," sighed Tiff. "By that chemist shop."

"Where?" Gran and I both spun around.

Anthony was back to full size, leaning against the shop with his arms crossed.

"What a time you must have had," cried Gran, rushing towards him. "Let's get you back to the boat for a nice cup of tea and a chat."

"Why is everyone making such a fuss?" said Tiff.

"It's nothing," I said.

I smiled at Anthony but he ignored me. It was probably best to leave him with Gran. I remembered how she'd made me feel better when I first told her I'd shrunk.

"So, did you find anything good for your Cleopatra costume?" I said, linking arms with Tiff.

"Yes." She opened a little paper bag and showed me an enormous pair of gold hoop earrings.

"They're perfect," I grinned. "Will you come and look in the chemist shop with me? I think they might have something good for my costume."

"In a chemist shop?" asked Tiff. "What are you going to do, dress up in a baby's nappy?"

"Not quite. We'll catch you up," I called after Anthony and Gran.

We were at the very edge of the market now. The chemist shop was pretty much like the stores we have in Swanchester, with plasters and soap and bottles of shampoo.

"Excuse me," I asked the man behind the counter, "do you have any bandages?"

"Bandages?" said Tiff.

"I want to dress up as an Ancient Egyptian mummy for the party," I explained. "Bandages will be much stronger than the toilet roll we used at home."

The chemist shook his head.

"Two elderly American ladies just left," he said. "They bought all my bandages. Every single roll."

"That must be the Calendar sisters," I said. "Do you think they want the bandages for the cats?"

"Or perhaps they're going to dress up as mummies like you," snorted Tiff.

"You're right," I cried. "Anthony and I just saw them buying huge bags of cinnamon and nutmeg. I bet they're even going to make themselves smell like they've been mummified in ancient spice."

"Gross!" squealed Tiff.

No imagination!

"The Ancient Egyptians always used scented oils and spices to preserve the bodies," I explained. "I think it's mummy-marvellous the sisters are going to make such an effort. I wish I'd thought of smelling like I'd been dead for thousands of years myself."

By the time Tiffany and I made it back to the boat, Gran and Anthony were already sitting out on the deck. Gran was smiling but Anthony had his back to her and was staring out at the Nile.

I got the feeling he was blaming Gran for passing shrinking down the family. Why couldn't he see what brilliant fun it was?

"Hi," I called out. "We're back."

Gran waved and so did Professor Gus, who was reading a big, thick book, wrapped up in brown paper, at a table nearby. Anthony didn't even look round.

As soon as we reached the top of the gangplank, Ozzy sidled over and wound himself around my ankles, purring.

"That cat worships you," said Professor Gus.

"And I like him too," I smiled, tickling Ozzy between the ears. He arched his back and jumped on to my shoulder in a single bound.

"You look like a pirate with a parrot," giggled Gran.

"Shiver me timbers," I said as Ozzy's tail tickled me under my nose.

"He still gives me the creeps," said Tiff, moving away.

"I think he's lovely," I said. "I'm not surprised the Ancient Egyptians thought cats were like gods . . . though don't tell Chip I said that."

"Quite so. Quite so," agreed the professor, gathering his big, brown-paper-covered book under his arm.

Anthony spun round. "I wish that cat wasn't even on this boat," he said. "I wish we could sail away and leave it behind."

"Anthony, for heaven's sake," scolded Gran.

"What a horrible thing to say," I cried … although I guessed Anthony was probably just worried Ozzy might eat him if he shrank.

Even Tiffany looked shocked and the Calendar sisters, who were coming up the gangplank laden with bags and packages, let out a cry.

"How cruel," they gasped, clinging to each other as if Anthony had actually taken Ozzy and flung him head first into the Nile.

Anthony didn't apologize. But he did look at his feet, blushing scarlet as if he realized it had been a pretty nasty thing to say.

Ozzy wasn't bothered at all, of course. He steadied himself on my shoulder and rubbed his head against my ear.

"Better watch out, Oz," I laughed, as his tail nearly went right up my nose. "Next stop – Temple of the Cats."

CHAPTER 16

We arrived at the site of the ancient temple early next morning. I ≡ **sped** on ahead as Anthony and Tiff walked up from the river behind me.

"Come on!" I called. I couldn't believe we'd reached the archeological dig at long last.

At first glance, the ruins didn't really look anything like a temple – just a flat, sandy field with piles of bricks and some broken pillars. But Miss June and Miss July were right. There must have been at least fifty or sixty stray cats. Lots of them were sleeping in the

shade of the broken stones but a few
kittens were scampering about on the
sand before the sun got too hot.

"The local people feed them a little," said Musa
as he joined us. "But it is a hard life."

"Thank goodness Miss June and Miss July are
here to help them," I said.

The two old ladies were already making

 their way around with a
watering can and saucers
to give the cats a drink.

"There's something
creepy about those Calendar sisters," said Anthony,
as Musa hurried on. "Like this morning when. . ."

"Honestly!" I interrupted.
"You just don't like them

because you're terrified of cats."

"And cats is *all* they ever talk about," groaned Tiffany.

"Well, I like cats," I said, crouching down as a grey-and-white-speckled stray sniffed the air and prowled closer to us.

Anthony backed away.

"What a beautiful puss," said Gran, catching up with us. "He looks like a snow leopard with those spots."

She was right. As he opened his mouth to yawn, the speckled cat really did look like a leopard cub trying to roar.

"There are about ten more just like him," I said, pointing to small groups of

other spotty strays, sunbathing on the ruins nearby.

"Maybe they're part Egyptian wildcat or something," said Gran. "They do look sort of ancient."

"Shoo!" said Anthony, hiding behind me as one of the speckled strays edged closer. "Surely you can see how dangerous they are, Violet?" he hissed in my ear. "What if we shrank? This lot would GOBBLE us up in no time."

Poor Anthony. He really was frightened. But before I could answer, Musa called us over to join the rest of the passengers from the boat.

"Time to get started," he said, handing us each an old toothbrush.

"I'm not cleaning my teeth with this. It's filthy," whispered Tiff, looking horrified.

"It's not for your teeth, silly," I giggled. "It's to

brush dirt off any ancient objects that we find on the dig."

Tiff wasn't the only one who looked as clueless as a fish with a pair of new shoes.

Louis and Lola L'Amour had turned up in bright white clothes which were bound to get filthy in five seconds flat. And as Signora Sipperetto jogged on the spot, I couldn't see her sitting still long enough to brush mud off a stone. Even Professor Gus looked a little out of place. Musa had to ask him twice not to step on a piece of ground which had been marked off with string.

"No need to tell *me* what to do," huffed the professor. "I have been on many important archaeological digs before, you know."

Musa nodded politely and led us across the

sand towards a tall, crumbling statue of a woman with the head of a cat.

"Wow!" I squeezed my way to the front of the group.

Anthony followed. "That must be Bastet," he said, his eyes sparkling with excitement under the brim of his baseball cap.

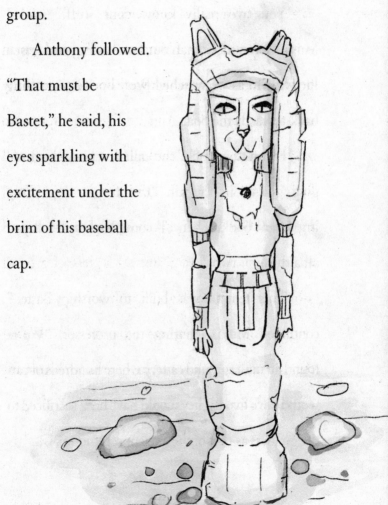

"The Ancient Egyptian cat goddess," I agreed. I'd read all about her in my *Bumper Book of Ancient Egypt*.

"You two really know your stuff," smiled Musa. "Even more than our famous Egyptologist." He winked as we watched Professor Gus scuttling back towards the boat.

"I won't be a tick," he called, waving his little gold glasses in the air. "I've forgotten my big important book. Then I'll come back and tell you all a thing or two."

"This temple was built to worship Bastet," continued Musa, ignoring the professor. "We've found an underground cattery where hundreds of cats would have lived. They would have been sacrificed to the goddess as part of the ancient ceremonies."

"Yikes! Don't let Ozzy go down there." I shuddered. "I don't think he'd like to know what happened to his poor pussycat ancestors."

"Luckily, Ozzy never comes ashore," laughed Musa, pointing back towards the *Cleopatra*. "He likes to stand guard in case any of the strays tries to visit the kitchens."

We could see the little ship's cat at the top of the gangplank trying to look tough, with his tail arched, as the professor hurried aboard.

"Are we going to dig in the underground cattery today?" I asked.

"No." Musa shook his head. "Work in that part of the temple has finished. We've closed it up again, in case it becomes unsafe. We're going to dig above ground, in the temple itself."

"Perfect." I grinned. I felt sure we would discover some dark and deadly spine-chilling Egyptian secrets. After all, this was the very place where the ancient cat-worshipping ceremonies used to take place.

Half an hour later, we'd all been given a demonstration of how to carefully sift through the sand, sweeping away the grains with our toothbrushes and looking for any ANCIENT EGYPTIAN remains underneath.

There were four or five big white tents scattered across the site to offer shade from the blazing sun as we worked.

Anthony and I were a little bit away from everyone else, inside a tent covering a stone slab that Musa told us would once have marked the temple's front door. By the end of the first hour, we'd already found three pieces of broken brown pottery.

"Not exactly a mummy's skull," I said. "But it's a start."

"Good work," said Musa, peering under the canvas to see how we were doing. "You have nearly found a whole bowl."

He lifted the pieces gently and showed us how they fitted together. "Keep looking," he called as he went off to help Tiffany.

"History Mystery Number One," I said in my best spooky voice. "I wonder if a temple cat drank out of this? Or perhaps Tutankhamun ate his Ancient Egyptian **CHOCCY-CHIMP** breakfast cereal from it."

"I love **CHOCCY-CHIMPS**," laughed Anthony. He really did sound happy and relaxed at long last.

"Me too!" I smiled, giving him a high five. "See? It's not *just* shrinking we have in common after all."

"I'm sorry I've been so grumpy," said Anthony, running sand through his fingers. "This has been my best day of the trip so far. It's really exciting . . . but we have to concentrate so hard, it's the first time I haven't been afraid that I'll shrink."

"I know what you mean," I agreed.

Anthony was smiling as he brushed away the sand from a piece of cracked pottery with his little red toothbrush. There was no sign of his phone or

"Wouldn't it be amazing if a crack suddenly opened up in the ground," I said, "and we fell down it, back thousands of years to Ancient Egypt."

"If we did time travel, we'd both be so excited we'd shrink straight away," laughed Anthony.

"Or we'd land in the cattery and the temple cats would gobble us the moment we arrived," I teased.

"Don't!" said Anthony, his eyes looking dark and worried for a moment. Then he smiled again.

It was so much fun talking to him like this. When he was relaxed he was just like the super-cool cousin I had always hoped he would be. Better than that, for the first time in my whole life, I had someone my own age I could imagine sharing

SHRINKING adventures with.

But we were interrupted as Professor Gus poked his head into the tent.

"Hello, Professor," said Anthony. "Can you tell us anything interesting about the goddess Bastet? After all, this temple is dedicated to her."

"Er ... well ... Bastet had the body of a woman and the paws of a cat," said the professor, nodding wisely

"*Paws?* Don't you mean the *head* of a cat?" asked Anthony, raising his eyebrows.

"Yes ... quite. Paws ... head ... maybe even a tail," said the professor, looking flustered. "That's just what I meant."

I looked over at Anthony and the two of us couldn't help giggling. I'd thought Professor Gus would have hundreds of brilliant stories and creepy facts about Ancient Egypt. But actually he was a BIG let-down. He was always boasting about how he was a world-famous Egyptologist, but he only ever seemed to know facts that he could have read about in a children's book.

"I . . . er . . . I'd better go and see if Musa needs me," he said, backing out of the tent. "I expect he could make use of my expert advice. . ."

"*Expert advice?*" snorted Anthony as the professor hurried away. "Musa knows far more about Ancient Egypt than he ever will."

"Even Mr Carl Moon knows more about Ancient Egypt than the professor," I giggled.

"Who's Mr Carl Moon?" asked Anthony.

I smiled as I told him about the funny American

Gran and I had met at the British Museum.

"He was a big, tall man, dressed like a cowboy," I explained. "He bought a copy of *The Bumper Book of Ancient Egypt* in the gift shop."

"I've seen that. It's a brilliant book," said Anthony.

"Exactly," I agreed. "So, if Mr Moon has read it, he will definitely know just as much as the professor by now."

CHAPTER 17

As soon as we came back to the boat that evening, I had a strange feeling that something was wrong.

The minute I sat down for dinner, I knew what it was.

"Where's Ozzy?" I said. "I haven't seen him since this morning."

Ever since our first night, he'd always curled himself around my ankles under the table because he knew I'd drop a few tasty scraps for him to eat.

"That's odd," agreed Musa. "I have never known him to disappear when there's food around."

Musa went down to the kitchens and Gran and I searched the deck but there was no sign of the beautiful grey cat anywhere.

"Oh dear," said Miss July, fanning herself with a napkin.

"I hope nothing terrible has happened to him," sniffed Miss June. Her eyes were all red and she looked as if she was about to cry.

Musa asked everyone to search their cabins. But there was no sign of Ozzy anywhere on board the *Cleopatra*.

"Perhaps he's jumped ship," said Signor Sipperetto.

"On a night like this, he has probably fallen in love with a beautiful stray," smiled Lola L'Amour, pointing up at the big full moon.

"I agree," said Louis. He kissed Lola's hand.

Yuck.

Musa paced up and down looking worried. "Ozzy has been the ship's cat ever since he was a kitten," he said. "We have visited this temple many times. I have never known him to leave the boat before. Ever."

"Not even to ... you know? To do his business?" I asked.

"Trust you to think of that, Violet," groaned Tiff. "You really are disgusting."

"Ozzy has a litter tray down by the store cupboard," said Musa. "I filled it with fresh sand just after breakfast. It has not been used since."

"You see," I cried, scowling at Tiff. What

did she know about being a detective? "Ozzy has definitely disappeared. If he hadn't he would have needed to go to the loo by now."

"We should send out a search party," said Gran. "Just in case he has gone to the ruins."

"But Musa said he never leaves the boat," frowned Anthony.

"I wouldn't go out in the dark if I was you," said Professor Gus, almost spilling his glass of after-dinner brandy. "I've been doing some research into this place and I've uncovered some very strange and creepy stories."

"I love spooky stories – the SCARIER the better," I said. "Especially if they're about a curse or the revenge of a hideous, headless mummy."

"This is a dark and grisly tale," said Professor

Gus, his voice booming across the deck. He really didn't know how to tell a scary story properly. He should have whispered if he really wanted to make a *SHIVER* run down our spines.

"It is believed that this place is haunted by a terrible blood-chilling curse. . ." he thundered, "the curse of a cat."

"A pussycat?" said Gran.

Anthony and I looked at each other. Surely the professor could do better than that? Tiffany giggled but Professor Gus ignored her.

"The first archaeologists who worked here would never go to the temple at night, all because of the terrible Curse of the Mummified Cat."

There was a gasp from both the Calendar sisters, who clutched each other's hands in horror.

Even Signora Sipperetto had stopped jiggling for a moment.

Perhaps this was going to be a good story after all – something only a true Egyptologist would know. I looked up at the full moon and tried the help the professor out a bit...

"Yowl!" I made my best attempt a gruesome kitty's howl.

"Shh!" The professor put his finger to his lips. "The archaeologists found that anyone who went to the temple after dark woke the next day with..."

"With what...?" urged Lola L'Amour.

"With whiskers on their face," said the professor. "It was as if they had been turned into cats in their sleep."

"That's horrible," gasped Tiffany. She wasn't

laughing now. She was terrified about getting a spot on her face so the thought of cat whiskers made her clutch her cheeks in horror.

Lola and Louis L'Amour looked worried too.

"One man woke up with furry ears," said the professor. "And a young Egyptian guide even grew a tail."

"Goodness me, Gus," sniggered Signor Sipperetto. "You'll give the children nightmares."

The professor might have managed to frighten the frizz out of Tiffany but I could tell from the grin on Anthony's face that he didn't believe a word. Neither did I. There weren't nearly enough popping eyeballs and green-tinged skin to scare us. Turning into a cat ... For goodness' sake! Hannibal my hamster could tell a better spooky story than this!

"I do not wish to frighten anyone," said Professor Gus, looking a little annoyed that Ant and I weren't shivering like wobbly jellies. "I just want to warn you all not to leave this boat after dark."

"Very wise," shuddered the Calendar sisters.

But Musa shrugged and unhooked a lantern from above the gangplank. "I have never heard these stories before," he said. "If you will excuse me, professor, I am going out to look for my lost cat."

CHAPTER 18

Gran and I were up before any of the other passengers next morning. We found Musa busy preparing the breakfast table. There was still no sign of Ozzy.

"He would never have left the boat by his own choice," said Musa. "I am certain of that."

"Then what can have happened to him?" asked Gran.

Musa looked as if he hadn't slept a wink. I couldn't bear to imagine how I'd feel if Chip went missing.

"Either there has been a terrible accident,"

said Musa, laying teacups and saucers on the buffet for breakfast. "Or somebody on this boat did something very bad to him."

"Bad?" said Gran. "You don't mean. . .?"

"I don't know," said Musa quickly. None of us wanted to think what the end of Gran's sentence might have been.

"Maybe someone stole him," I said. "He is a very beautiful cat."

"Perhaps," said Musa sadly.

Gran and I looked at each other as he went back down to the kitchen. Did someone on the boat really know what had happened to Ozzy? Had they hurt him somehow or hidden him away somewhere? Who would do a thing like that?

"It's like a proper whodunit," said Gran.

"If only I could shrink," I whispered. "Being tiny always makes it so much easier to creep about and find out what's *really* going on."

"No more pickles for you then," said Gran, squeezing my hand.

"Poor Ozzy. I've grown to love that cat," I said.

"At least we know it wasn't you who did something to him," said Gran. She looked over at the eleven teacups Musa had spread out on the buffet table. One for every passenger. She took the teacup nearest to her and turned it over so that it was upside down in the saucer. "There. That's you counted out, Violet."

I saw what she was doing at once. "Tumbling temples, you're brilliant, Gran!" I said. Each passenger on the *Cleopatra* was represented by a teacup. We just had to keep turning them over

until we saw who was left.

"It definitely wasn't you either," I said turning

over the next cup.

"It's just like solving a puzzle," winked Gran.

"It wasn't Tiff," I said, turning over another one. "She might be a fluffy-haired, mirror-mad flea-brain sometimes but she would never do anything mean to an animal."

"And it wasn't Anthony," said Gran.

But my hand shot out towards the cup before she could turn it over.

"I'm not so sure," I said.

It was tummy-twistingly awful to think that Anthony might be the criminal but I couldn't ignore the feeling that was churning in my gut.

"He hates cats. Do you remember when we came back from the market?" I asked. "He said he wished that Ozzy wasn't even on this boat."

"I did think that was strange," said Gran. "He has two cats of his own at home. Cocoa and

Caramel. He used to send me pictures he'd drawn of them when he was little."

"Shrinking's changed him," I said. "He's terrified. You saw how worried he was when we were near the spotty strays. I bet he's scared that if he shrinks on board the boat, Ozzy will eat him."

Gran looked pale. "I really *don't* think it's Anthony," she said. But I still had my hand on the cup and she didn't try to turn it over.

"How about Signor Sipperetto?" she asked.

"I've seen him stroking Ozzy a zillion times. He loves cats," I said.

"Ah . . . so does he love Ozzy enough to steal him for himself?" asked Gran.

"No." I turned Signor Sipperetto's cup over. "No one who really cares for an animal would ever try and take it away from a happy home."

"True. And it wasn't Signora Sipperetto either," said Gran. "She's too busy thinking about herself and keeping fit to even notice a cat."

"And Lola and Louis L'Amour are too busy thinking about each other," I said, turning over their cups and blushing pink as a raspberry as I thought about how they were always kissing. "And it definitely wasn't the Calendar sisters. They're far too crazy about cats to want to harm Ozzy in any way."

"Agreed," said Gran, and we flipped their cups over too.

"So that just leaves the professor," I said.

"...That just leaves the professor for *what*?" boomed a posh voice right behind my ear.

I spun around to see Professor Gus leaning

on the back of my chair.

How long had he been standing there? How much had he heard?

"Erm," I said helplessly.

"That just leaves the professor . . . to see if he wants tea or coffee this morning," smiled Gran. "Musa was wondering how many of each he should make and we were trying to guess. Weren't we, Violet?"

"Er . . . yes," I said, nodding so hard it must have looked as if my head was on a bouncy spring.

Gran is amazing. She might be a little old lady but she thinks so fast her brain is like a skiddy motorbike on a race track.

"I'll have English tea, please," said Professor Gus.

Gran pushed his empty cup towards him.

We still hadn't turned it over.

There was definitely something not quite right about the professor... That silly ghost story last night that Musa said he had never heard before. And the way, for a world-famous history whizz, it always seemed as if he had just read his facts from *The Bumper Book of Ancient Egypt*. But what did any of that have to do with a missing cat?

I glanced down at the table. There were only two cups we had not turned over.

One was for the professor . . . the other was for Anthony.

The sun was baking hot already this morning but a cold shiver ran down my spine. Did either Anthony or Professor Gus really know what had happened to Ozzy?

CHAPTER 19

All day long I kept a lookout for Ozzy and I watched Anthony as we worked together on the dig. If he really did know something about the missing cat, he didn't show any sign of it.

He seemed totally relaxed as he raked through the sand, talking happily about how much fun teeny-tiny time travel would be if only we could SHRINK and go back to Ancient Egypt. We imagined creeping about trying not be squashed by giant stones as the pyramids were built.

Tiffany refused to come back to the dig. "This is our last day on the boat," she said. "If I want to look beautiful when I dress up as Cleopatra for the party tonight I need to have perfect skin."

"What *is* she doing?" asked Anthony as we watched her tiptoeing down to the edge of the river with one of the little plastic pots I had used to keep my pickles in.

"Nile mud," I said. "I told her it was good for her face. It's the whole reason she came to Egypt in the first place."

"Oh dear. Mum uses mud packs sometimes," laughed Anthony, "but I don't think you're supposed to scoop it out of the river like that."

"Probably not," I grinned.

Gran had said she was stiff from digging

yesterday so she was going to stay on the boat too. She'd promised to try and make a pharaoh mask for Anthony to wear at the party.

"Not that I am much good at art and craft," she told me. "But I am determined to try and keep Anthony cheerful."

"And I've got my costume sorted too," I grinned.

Musa had given me some rolls of bandage from the boat's first-aid kit, so I could dress up as a mummy after all.

"I'm going to look like a giant, life-size version of my key ring, and you'll look like your pharaoh one," I said to Anthony as we were digging.

"Ha," Anthony laughed. "It's strange to think this will be our last night on the *Cleopatra*, isn't it?"

"Just so long as we find Ozzy before we go," I said.

"I hope we do too," said Anthony.

I wanted more than ever to believe that he didn't know where the little cat had gone.

"Have you noticed," he said, "there are fewer strays today? All those spotty ones that look like leopard cubs. The ones Gran likes. . ."

"They're gone!" I said.

Anthony was right. Although there were plenty of ordinary-looking black and tabby strays dozing in the sun, there was not a speckled cat to be seen anywhere.

I didn't see a single one in the ruins all day. And there was no sign of Ozzy either.

*

When I had finished digging, I searched all round the temple and up and down the riverbank for the little missing cat.

When I returned to the *Cleopatra* I saw Musa carrying tables down to the edge of the water ready for the barbecue.

"I can't imagine where poor Ozzy has disappeared to," he said, shaking his head sadly.

"Don't worry. We *will* find him," I said.

I dashed back to the cabin with just half an hour to spare before the party. The minute I opened the door, Tiffany leapt at me, wailing like a zombie. "VIOLET, look what you've done," she howled. "That stinky Nile mud has brought me out in blotches."

Poor Tiff. Her face was covered in a bright

red rash. One minute she was pea-green from feeling seasick . . . now she had more spots than my polka-dot trousers.

"I don't look anything like Cleopatra," she wailed. "I look more like. . ."

"Cleo-SPLAT-ra?" I said, trying not to laugh.

Tiffany threw herself on the bed. "Professor Gus was right," she sobbed. "There *is* a curse."

"You didn't even go outside after dark," I said. "And anyway, he said you'd grow whiskers, not spots."

"This is all your fault ... *as usual*," growled Tiffany.

"We'll just have to make the best of it," I said, sitting down next to her and helping her rub some white make-up on her cheeks.

"Wow!" I said. The pale cream made the black lines she'd drawn around her eyes look really dark and glamorous. By the time she'd put on the big gold earrings she'd bought at the market and a sparkly sequin dress from home, she actually looked pretty cool.

"Totally Cleo-tastic!" I said, twirling her around in front of the mirror.

What we didn't know was that Lola L'Amour had decided to come to the party dressed as Cleopatra too.

I thought Tiffany might run back to our cabin as we stepped off the boat and saw the beautiful young bride in a black shiny wig.

But Tiff threw back her shoulders. "Here goes," she said. "It's not every day you get to share the same style as a Paris fashion model."

"Good for her," winked Gran from behind a pair of very long false eyelashes she had managed to find for her camel costume. "And I see you've wrapped up nicely, Violet," she laughed, adjusting the hump on her back.

"Tiffany helped," I said, spinning around so that Gran could see my bandages from all sides. "We had a bit of practice with some toilet rolls before we left home."

I waved at Tiffany. She looked as if

she was going to faint as Louis L'Amour – who was dressed as an Ancient Egyptian soldier with nothing but a tea towel tied around his waist – took pictures of her and Lola on his phone.

"Bet that's going to go Tiff's social-face-thingy page," laughed Gran.

"And the Calendar sisters are going to be dressed as mummies, just like me," I said, explaining to Gran how they had bought loads of bandages and spice at the market. "They're even going to pong perfectly of cinnamon."

"Really? They told me they were going to come as cats," said Gran. "After all, that *is* what the fundraiser's for."

Sure enough, I saw the sisters approaching along the riverbank in the lantern light. Each had a little pair of pointy ears attached to a headband and a tabby tail bobbing along behind her.

"Strange," I muttered. "What can they have wanted the spice and bandages for?"

Before Gran could answer, Professor Gus appeared. He was dressed like an old-fashioned explorer with big baggy shorts, showing off his *very* knobbly knees.

"Tell me, Professor," said Gran with a naughty twinkle in her eye, "do you think it is safe for us to be standing here in the dark like this? I mean, we are outside. . ."

"If you're talking about the curse," said Professor Gus rather crossly, "I think you'll be all right as long as you stay close to the boat. But don't go anywhere near the temple."

"It's too late," I giggled, glancing at the Calendar sisters with their tails wrapped neatly over their arms. "I am afraid to say Miss June and Miss July have already been down to the temple tonight. I have proof."

"What do you mean?" Professor Gus turned white. "Where did you see them go?"

He looked so panicked I felt bad for teasing him.

"I was only joking," I mumbled, pointing to the sisters' tabby ears. "...I was pretending they'd been turned into cats, you see."

"Laugh all you like," said the professor. "But do NOT go near those ruins tonight ... not to any part of the temple, especially the underground cattery ... or you WILL be struck by the curse."

"Careful!" cried Gran as he stormed away,

bumping into Anthony and almost tipping him into the river.

"Wow!" I gasped as I caught hold of Anthony's arm and saved him. "What a totally cool costume!"

Anthony was dressed in blue pyjama trousers and a blue T-shirt, which Gran had sewn a gold trim on to.

Most amazing of all was his Egyptian headdress. It was blue and gold with a cobra rising up in the centre.

"You look like a real pharaoh," I grinned.

"It's only cardboard and paint," said Anthony. "Louis L'Amour made it for me. That's his job. He makes props and things for fashion shoots. That's where he first met Lola."

"You promised you'd say I made the costume all by myself, without any help from the professionals," laughed Gran.

"You did ... of course ... completely," fibbed Anthony as Gran hugged us both.

"Isn't this the nicest Nile night ever," I sighed.

Here we were, standing on the banks of the river, our nostrils filled with yummy smells of barbecue as a band of Egyptian musicians played harps and pipes under a perfect full moon.

"It's amazing," said Anthony, doing a funny pharaoh dance and giving me a high five. I hoped more than ever that he didn't know anything about where Ozzy had gone.

"It's a wonderful evening," Gran agreed. "And it was all your idea, Violet."

I could see the Calendar sisters grinning from ear to ear as they collected donations for CLAW from the wealthy passengers who were standing around sipping glasses of champagne.

"Please give generously," cried Miss June, shaking a bucket under Signor Sipperetto's nose (or snout, I should say, because he was dressed as a crocodile).

"I just wish Ozzy was here," I sighed. "Everything would be totally perfect, if only we could find him tonight."

CHAPTER 20

Later that evening, when the party was almost over, Gran found me sitting on the gangplank of the *Cleopatra* throwing stones into the water.

"Come on," she said, taking two lanterns from the side of the boat. "Follow me."

"Where are we going?" I asked.

"To look for Ozzy," said Gran. "That's what you're sitting here wishing you could do, isn't it?"

"He's not on the boat, so he must be somewhere out there," I said, pointing towards the ruins. "It's our last chance to find him. Musa has to sail back for more tourists tomorrow and we're heading home."

"What are we waiting for then?" said Gran. "Let's go."

"You're the best," I said, slipping my hand into hers. I knew Mum and Dad would never let me wander round a spooky tumbledown temple at night.

"Should we tell Tiff and Anthony where we're going?" I asked.

"Tiff's gone to bed," said Gran. "I think she wanted to get as much beauty sleep as she could after the incident with the mud rash."

"Oh dear," I giggled. "And where's Anthony?"

"I haven't seen him for a while," said Gran.

"But I told Musa to keep a lookout for him. We won't be very long."

"Did you tell Musa where we were going?" I asked.

"No," said Gran. "Perhaps I should have done. But I didn't want to get his hopes up."

"Wouldn't it be totally brilliant if we came back carrying Ozzy?" I grinned.

"One thing," whispered Gran, "if that curse is true and I sprout whiskers, I'm blaming you."

"We must make a pretty funny sight in our costumes," I hissed as we tiptoed across the sand. "A camel and a mummy on a midnight stroll."

"I'd forgotten I was still wearing my hump," laughed Gran. "But don't worry, no one can see us."

"They can see our lanterns," I said, wishing we'd been more careful about showing our lights. I don't know why but I didn't want everyone to know we had come to look for Ozzy out here.

"Where to first?" asked Gran.

"I'm not sure," I said, suddenly feeling hopeless. "I've already looked around the temple ruins a zillion times in the daylight."

"Well, let's think logically," said Gran. "Where might Ozzy wander off to? Or where might someone take a cat if they wanted him to be hidden?"

"The ancient cattery," I said – and as soon as I opened my mouth, I knew I was right. I remembered how Musa had described the maze of underground rooms and tunnels where the temple cats were kept all those thousands of years ago. "I can't believe I didn't think of it before," I cried. "That is just the sort of place Ozzy would be trapped."

"Nobody's even mentioned it since that first day when Musa told us it was all closed up," said Gran, shrugging. Her camel hump wobbled in the darkness ahead of me.

"No," I cried, breaking into a run. "You're wrong. Professor Gus mentioned it just now. Remember? When he was warning us about the curse. He said don't go to the temple – *especially* not the underground cattery. . . It was like he was making a point to keep us away."

I ran on past Gran. "Hurry," I called over my shoulder.

I sprinted away so fast I jiggled my lantern and it went out. I stood panting at the top of a steep slope as Gran caught up and shone her light on me.

"Ozzy is in that cattery," I said. "I am sure of it. And I think Professor Gus put him there."

"I know you don't trust him," said Gran. "But. . ."

"That's what that crazy curse story was all about," I said. "He was making sure we'd keep away. Especially kind people like the Calendar sisters. They were desperate to go out and look for Ozzy but they're easily scared."

"Why would he go to all that trouble just for one little cat?" said Gran.

"I don't know. But that's what we're going to find out," I said. My tummy was popping with excitement.

Gran held her lantern higher.

We were standing close to the edge of a deep pit. "If we could just get down there, perhaps we would find a way to get underground," I said.

"I think we should go back and get help," said

Gran. "At least fetch a ladder."

"Fine," I said. I knew Gran was right. But my fingers and toes were fizzing like sherbet . . . I wanted to find a way into the tunnels of the cattery *right now*.

Then two things happened very fast and at almost exactly the same time.

WHOOSH!

I shrank to the size of a tiny *shabti*.

And Gran stumbled forward.

"Help!" she cried as her foot SLIPPED on the sharp stones. Her giant-sized shoe shot towards me like a speed boat out of control.

"Yikes!"

"Look out!" gasped Gran as she accidentally kicked me up in the air. . .

Wheeee!

I felt as if I was falling from the top of a steep cliff as we both came tumbling down into the deep pit below.

"Ouch," cried Gran as she hit the bottom.

"Ouch," I cried as I landed beside her. Luckily something soft broke my fall. I think it must have been Gran's camel hump.

The moon had gone behind a cloud. I couldn't see anything at all but I could hear Gran breathing beside me.

"Are you all right?" I asked, crawling close to where I thought Gran's ear must be. "Did you drop your lantern when you fell?"

"That's just it, Violet," whispered Gran in the darkness. "I didn't fall . . . I was pushed."

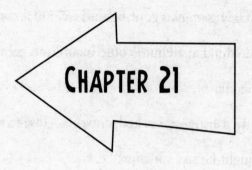

CHAPTER 21

As the moon came out from behind a cloud, the deep pit was flooded with light. I could see that Gran was biting her lip as she lay slumped on the floor beside me.

"It's my ankle," she winced. "I think it may be broken."

"Oh no," I panicked. What could I do? I was no bigger than a sticking plaster. "If only I was still full size. Then at least we could use the bandages from my mummy costume to wrap around your foot."

I looked helplessly at my outfit. Each bandage

was only as thick as a shoelace now I'd shrunk.

I stood on tiptoes, feeling like a tiny frog trapped in the bottom of a well. My heart beating loudly, I listened in case anyone was still moving about at the top of the pit.

The only noise was the distant music from the party. It sounded so faint it could have been a zillion miles away.

"I don't think there's any sign of the person who pushed you," I whispered.

"Whoever it was will be long gone by now," said Gran. "They wanted us out of the way down here . . . or me, at least. I don't suppose they even saw you."

"I bet it was Professor Gus," I said. "He's always been our main suspect for taking Ozzy."

Unless. . . A terrible thought struck me.

Anthony wouldn't have done this to Gran, would he?

No.

I was sure he hadn't.

"You explore the pit and see if there's a way out of here," said Gran. "I'll shout for help. If anyone comes, jump in my pocket and they won't see you."

"OK." I scuttled away across the sandy floor like a scarab beetle.

"HELP!" hollered Gran at the top of her lungs. "PLEASE, HELP US!"

I don't know how long Gran shouted for but it felt like hours.

No one came.

The walls of the ancient pit were made from big flat stones. There was no entrance to the cattery down here after all. I tried again and again to get my footing so I could climb out. But it was hopeless. It was like trying to escape from the deep end of an empty swimming pool – the walls were just too steep and slippery.

"There's a tiny gap between two stones in the corner," I said, swinging myself on to Gran's sleeve and scrambling up to her shoulder so she could hear me. "I think it might be a mouse hole. I'm going to see where it leads. Perhaps I can get out on the other side and run for help."

"All right," said Gran. She was still lying on her side. "Find Anthony. It won't matter if he sees you while you're tiny. He can tell someone I'm down here."

"I will," I said. It made me feel better to know that Gran trusted Anthony.

"Be careful," she said. "And turn back if there's any sign of danger."

"Don't worry," I said, sliding down her sleeve and doing a mini super hero pose to try and make her smile.

"Violet Potts to the rescue," I cried, skidding away and squeezing into the narrow hole.

"Ahhhhhhhhhhhhhhhhhh!" I had expected to find a tunnel on the other side of the gap . . . or some sort of little mousey burrow . . . but there was nothing. No floor at all.

Wheeee!

I **PLUNGED** down like one of those little plastic airman you get in joke shops and party bags.

Except I didn't have a parachute, of course.

Flump!

I landed on a pile of sand and sank to my waist like a teaspoon in a sugar bowl.

I looked up and saw the tiny gap I had fallen through like a keyhole high above me.

There was no way I was going to get back through there again. I would have to find another way out if I was going to get help for Gran.

I looked around and saw that I had fallen into some sort of long corridor or passageway. The roof and walls were made of stone. Every few metres or so there were little piles of sand like the one I had fallen into. They had probably been made by the archaeologists when they were digging here.

This must be the ancient cattery, I thought. *This corridor probably leads to the rooms where the temple cats were kept.*

I slid down the pile of sand and looked up at the brightly lit walls all around me.

Brightly lit. . . It took me a moment to realize what was wrong. It was the middle of the night. I was in an underground chamber. It should have been pitch black down here. Instead, a string of light bulbs on thick electrical cord were blazing above my head as high as street lamps.

Someone else must be down here with me.

Someone else must have turned these lights on.

I crept forward and looked in both directions.

The passageway was empty.

Which way should I go? I stood frozen like a mouse on a train track.

"MAW." A noise pierced the darkness.

It sounded like a baby crying.

"MAW, MAAAAAW."

No. Not a baby. I felt my heart jump like a tree frog inside my chest.

"Ozzy," I whispered.

I'd recognize that yowling anywhere.

"MAAAAAAAAW."

I darted forward in the direction the sound was coming from.

The corridor started to really wind now,

ZIGZAGGING like the clues in a wordsearch puzzle. I was so tiny it took ages to run a distance that would only have been two or three footsteps if I was full size.

Panting like a marathon runner, I turned a sharp corner and skidded to a stop.

"What are you doing here?" I gasped as a little figure the size of a chess piece blocked my path.

Anthony was standing in front of me. He was as small as I was. He looked like an action figure, wearing his shrunken pharaoh outfit, with his hands held out to stop me.

"Get back," he hissed.

"MAAAW." Ozzy's cry echoed off the stone walls.

"I am not going anywhere, Anthony," I said. "Not until I find out what you've done to that poor cat."

CHAPTER 22

Anthony dodged sideways and blocked my path again.

"I haven't done anything to Ozzy," he said, his tiny eyes almost popping out of his head. "I was frightened of him in case I shrank but I would never hurt an animal. I love cats. I've got two of my own at home."

"Then what are you doing down here?" I said. "Why are you trying to stop me?"

"I slipped away from the party," said Anthony, pulling me into the shadows close to the wall. "I heard Professor Gus warning you and Gran not to come to the cattery. I knew he must have hidden Ozzy down here. I had to come and look."

I could tell at once that Anthony was telling the truth.

"I can't go on being frightened to do things just in case I shrink," he said. "And I didn't want Gran coming down here in the dark. It's not safe."

"But she did come," I groaned. "And now she's badly hurt."

I explained what had happened and how we needed to find someone who could rescue Gran from the deep pit.

"We're about as useful as two toy soldiers against a real army," sighed Anthony. "I tried my best not to shrink but one look at this place and ... whoosh." Anthony waved his little arms and pointed to the tunnel around us. "It was amazing. I came in through this decorated room – with hieroglyphs and hundreds of tiny pictures of cats."

"So there is another way out of here. Show me," I said. "We need to get help. Once people come, they can look for Ozzy too."

I grabbed Anthony's sleeve and tried to drag him forward but he dug his heels into the sand.

"It's like a maze down here," he said.

"Well, you ought to be good at that. Just like your computer game," I said, dashing forward again.

"It's a dead end that way. I've already looked," said Anthony, pointing left along the corridor. "But I'm not sure we can get back the way I came."

"Mouldy mummies, of course we can," I said.

Before Anthony could stop me, I turned right along the passageway and began to run.

"Please, Violet. Wait." Anthony caught up with me. "I saw someone down here. It looked like. . ."

Suddenly a giant shadow fell across our path.

"Professor Gus!" I whispered, grabbing Anthony and leaping back into the gloom.

The professor came hurrying through an archway in the wall and dashed ahead of us along the passage.

"Hurry up, girls. We ain't got all night," he boomed.

"That's funny..." I cocked my head. "He doesn't sound like Professor Gus. He sounds..."

"American, I know. That's what I've been trying to tell you," hissed Anthony. "I'm not sure that is the professor. It looks like him but..."

"...it doesn't sound like him," I said as a voice like a cowboy echoed through the tunnels again.

"We need to finish before dawn if we want to meet that idiot antiques dealer at the railroad station," he boomed.

"This doesn't make any sense," I whispered, scuttling forward and pulling Anthony with me. "I recognize that voice. It belongs to ... Carl Moon. He's the American man I told you about. The one Gran and I met at the British Museum."

I peeped around the corner to see the big man crouching on the floor and winding up a trail of tangled bandages. He was still wearing the explorer costume the professor had on at the party.

"That's definitely Carl Moon," I whispered. "Except then he had a long moustache and a cowboy hat. He must have shaved off the moustache and put on a posh English voice and a pair of glasses."

"Then who is he really?" asked Anthony.

"No idea," I said. "But one thing is certain. Carl Moon and Professor Gus are the same person."

"Sorry, girls. I had to take care of a little business," shouted the professor (it was easier to think of him like that). He finished winding up the bandages and hurried away in the direction he'd been calling. Who could he be shouting to?

"MAAAW."

"And keep that darn cat quiet," he bellowed.

"Come on, let's follow him," said Anthony.

"And find Ozzy," I nodded.

We scampered forward, keeping to the shadows at the edge of the corridor like two tiny mice.

"Anthony," I hissed, wrinkling my nose. "Is it just me or does it smell funny down here? Like . . . Christmas."

Before Anthony could answer, we both skidded to a stop.

We had arrived at the entrance of a huge underground cavern. Standing in the middle of the stone room, each wearing a big black leather apron over the top of their cat costumes, were Miss June and Miss July.

"What are they doing here?" hissed Anthony.

Miss June was stirring a giant saucepan, which looked almost like a witch's cauldron. It was bubbling away on top of a big, flat camping stove.

"Cinnamon! That must be where the smell is coming from,"

I said, creeping forward.

Anthony and I slipped behind a broken wooden crate.

Just in front of us, Miss July was laying bandages out on a long table.

"You dropped these in the passageway," said the professor. He handed her the baggy rolls we'd seen him winding up outside.

"Why, thank you, August dear," said Miss July in her thick American accent.

"Just keep it speedy, will ya?" shrugged the professor.

"August?" Anthony whispered.

"Of course. June, July and August! I can't believe I've been so stupid," I said, burying my tiny head in my hands. "He must be their brother."

As I looked up at two plump ladies and the

man we had thought was the professor, I saw that all three had the same chunky build and broad shoulders.

"Gus is short for August," I groaned. "The Calendar sisters told me they had a brother with that name."

I thought of how Gran and I had been stuck on the *SOLVE IT!* wordsearch because we'd been looking for the long name, Tutankhamun, while the pharaoh's nickname, Tut, was in front of us all along.

"The three of them do look pretty alike," said Anthony. "And they sound alike now too. But with that fake English accent, I would never have guessed Professor Gus was the Calendar sisters' brother."

"But what are they doing here?" I asked. "That's what I want to know."

I glanced around the huge room, trying to take it all in.

The ceiling was hung with electric lights and I could see that hundreds of big square holes had been carved into the stone walls. They were almost like boxes in a pet shop.

This must be where the Ancient Egyptians kept the cats, I thought.

"MAW, MAAAAAW."

Anthony and I shot up on tiptoes at exactly the same time.

Someone had put a metal cage inside one of the ancient cat holes and Ozzy was staring out at us. "We've found him," I grinned, squeezing Anthony's hand.

"Achoo," Miss June SNEEZED. "I tell you something," she said. "I ain't touchin' that lot.

They bring out my allergies."

I looked up, following the direction that she was pointing in.

Ten more of the cat holes, opposite Ozzy's, were filled with cages too.

"Look, it's the spotty strays," whispered Anthony.

"But why are they shut up in here?" I said, my tummy tightening like a fist. "I thought the Calendar sisters loved cats. What are the bandages for and why are they boiling spices in the middle of the night?"

"Achoo," Miss June SNEEZED again. "Now my eyes are running too," she said, wiping her cheeks.

I remembered how she'd thrown Ozzy off her lap, pretending he was hurting her sore knee. But now I could see the truth. She couldn't bear him to be near her because she was allergic to cats. . . The Calendar sisters definitely weren't the sweet little old ladies I'd thought they were.

"Anthony," I whispered, edging forward around the side of the wooden crate. "Something really bad is going on here."

"I ain't touching those cats when we take 'em out to the boat," said Miss June, blowing her nose loudly on the end of her tabby fancy dress tail.

"Quit your fussing," said Miss July. "By the time we head out of here, those cats will be wrapped up in bandages and smelling of cinnamon."

"Ready to sell as ancient artefacts to that ignorant young dealer," grinned Professor Gus.

I looked around the cavern. First at the bandages. Then at the bubbling pot of spice. Last of all at Ozzy and the speckled strays, trapped in their cages.

"Anthony," I said gripping his arm. "I know what's going on here . . . Professor Gus and his sisters are going to mummify these cats."

CHAPTER 23

My tiny head was spinning as I tried to make sense of everything I had seen and heard. The Calendar sisters weren't kind little old ladies who loved cats . . . they were criminals, just like their brother August.

I realized Gus – or Carl Moon, as he was pretending to be then – must have visited the British Museum to find out as much as he could about Ancient Egypt. Now he was passing himself off as a professor – but he didn't know much more than he'd read in his *Bumper Book of Ancient Egypt*.

His silly story about the ancient curse was a trick, so everyone would stay away from the cattery.

I felt sick. "It's all my fault he came up with his horrible plan in the first place," I croaked. "I showed him the cat mummies at the British Museum. That's how he realized he could make a fortune selling fake mummies and pretending they're the real thing."

"The mummies may be fake," gulped Anthony, "but unless we do something quick, there'll be real cats inside them."

"That's why they stole Ozzy," I gasped. "He'd make a beautiful mummy..." I stopped myself. "I don't mean that the way it sounds." The thought of Ozzy being wrapped up in spice-scented bandages made my throat feel so tight I could barely breathe.

"I know what you're saying," agreed Anthony. "The whole idea of Ozzy being a mummy is horrible... but he would make a pretty brilliant one. He practically looks like an Egyptian god."

"And the speckled strays are like ancient wild cats," I said. "That's why the Calendar Gang left the ordinary, modern-shaped moggies alone."

"They don't need many mummies to sell anyway," said Anthony. "Each one will be worth a fortune if they can convince an antique dealer they're really from the time of the pharaohs."

"The spices will help with that," I said, watching Miss June dip rolls of bandage into the bubbling pot of cinnamon and nutmeg. "When I did my Egyptian project at school, I soaked it in tea to make it look like it was written on ancient papyrus paper. The spicy mixture will make the bandages turn brown and they'll look really old."

"A proper museum could tell they are fake immediately," said Anthony. "But it sounds like Calendar Gang plan on selling them to some greedy dealer and making a quick getaway."

"Come on," I said, as Miss June slopped another

roll of bandages into the bubbling pot. "We may be tiny but we have to think of a way to save these cats."

"Ready?" I said.

Anthony and I were standing under the **wobbly** legs of the camping stove. It towered above us like a roaring volcano.

Apparently, in stage ten of Maze of the Mummy, there's a bit where you have to escape from molten lava as it crashes through the floor of a tomb.

"We can do the same thing in real life . . . just as long as we run fast enough," Anthony promised me.

"Attack!" I cried.

We threw ourselves forward, charging at the leg of the stove with a wooden spoon we'd found on the floor. We held it out in front of us like a battering ram or a knight's lance.

CREAK!

The leg **wobbled** and. . .

CRASH!

The pot of steaming liquid fell to the floor.

"Look what you've done, June," August yelled

at his sister as she leapt out of the way of the stove.

"It worked!" Anthony cried as we fled from the

boiling, spicy liquid.

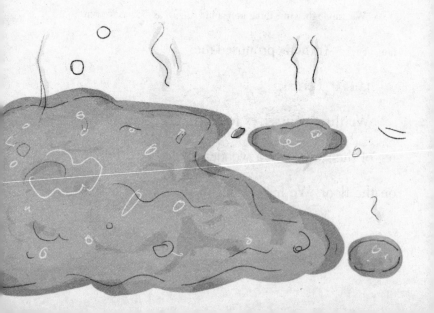

"Level complete! One zillion bonus points," I cheered.

We skidded to safety under the table.

"I'm beginning to enjoy this," Anthony panted.

"For someone who's scared of shrinking, you're actually pretty brave," I grinned. "Now all we've got to do is climb up the walls and free those cats."

"Easy," said Anthony. He sounded calm but he was shaking so hard the paper cobra on his headdress shook like a miniature rattlesnake.

"There's not a moment to lose," I said, glancing out from behind the table leg. The Calendar Gang were madly trying to mop up the spilled liquid. We'd have a couple of minutes' head start before they noticed what was going on.

"I'll undo Ozzy's cage. You start on the wildcats," I said. "Just fling open each door and move on to the next one as quick as you can."

"Got it," said Anthony.

He dashed across the floor and began to climb towards the strays without even looking back.

I headed up the wall to Ozzy.

The rough stones of the cavern made climbing pretty easy. I felt like one of the thumb-sized gecko lizards I'd seen scampering up the ruins while we were working on the dig. By fanning out my tiny hands – just like a lizard spreads its toes – I was able to cling on tight to the wall and move quickly upwards.

I was scared that Ozzy's cage would have a padlock or a tough bolt on the front. But there was actually just a bent nail hooked through the latch.

"Hi-ya!" With one good karate kick, I was able to bounce the nail free. "Go on, Ozzy, get out," I urged, swinging past him as the door opened.

I glanced over at Anthony. He had already opened four of the ten wildcat cages.

"Good going," I whistled.

Doing my best not to look down, I scampered along a narrow ledge on the wall to help him.

"Like tomb doors in The Maze!" he grinned.

In no time at all we had opened every cage.

I glanced down.

"Whoa!" My head swam for a moment – it was like the time I was about to leap from the highest treetop wire at the Monkey Business Adventure Park, when Uncle Max took me last half term.

At least we were so high up, the Calendar Gang still hadn't seen a thing.

Miss June had slipped on the spilled liquid. August and July were sniggering as they tried to heave her to her feet.

"Now what?" said Anthony.

I thought the minute we opened the cages the cats would spring out, but the strays were cowering inside, terrified by all the noise the Calendar Gang were making down below.

Even Ozzy, who was tame, had only poked his nose out of the front of his cage.

"What are we going to do?" said Anthony. "The cats won't move."

"There's only one thing we can do..." I said, "pretend to be mice so they chase us."

"You must be crazy," said Anthony. But he followed me as I scrambled down the wall and darted back and forward across the sandy floor like a mouse.

I glanced up and saw a row of emerald-green cats' eyes staring down at us.

"Yikes," squealed Miss July, she must have spotted us dashing across the floor. "Was that some kind of vermin?"

"Where'd it go?" Miss June leapt on to the table, her huge bottom making the whole thing sway underneath her. "Was it a snake or a rat?"

"Pull yourselves together, darn it," cried

August. "Can't you see the cats are escaping?"

As soon as they had jumped from their cages, the strays realized they were free and were dashing towards the doorway of the cavern. As I darted behind a table leg, I saw Ozzy drop gracefully to the floor and stalk among them with his nose in the air.

"Catch 'em. Herd 'em up," cried August.

But it was hopeless. There were too many cats. And they were far too quick to be caught.

"Hooray, they're getting away," I cried as I rolled under the crate and crouched down beside Anthony, who was already hiding there.

The ten strays sped off down the corridor.

"They'll be able to get out the same way I came in," grinned Anthony.

"Past the cat hieroglyphs," I laughed. "Perhaps in Ancient Egyptian the writing says EXIT THIS WAY."

"Chase after them, August," screamed June.

But August was wheezing. "I ain't fast enough," he sighed.

"At least we've still got that one. Look," said July.

Ozzy was the only cat who had not run away.

"Shoo!" I hissed, throwing a tiny stone at him.

"What was that?" said Miss June, peering down at the crate. "Something's under there, for sure."

Anthony and I stood as still as two wax crayons in a pencil box.

"It might be that snake," said Miss July.

"Yikes!" Miss June leapt backwards.

"Never mind that. I've got the cat!" cheered August. He was holding Ozzy high in the air by the scruff of his neck. "This one's the prettiest of them all," he grinned.

CHAPTER 24

Ozzy wriggled, desperately trying to escape as August squeezed his throat.

I closed my eyes.

This is it, I thought. People say cats have nine lives they can use up before they die – but Ozzy must have used his last one this time.

I was so tiny, there was nothing I could do to help.

"MAAAW."

A terrible, ear-splitting yowl echoed around the cavern.

I opened my eyes as Ozzy's front paw flashed through the air, scratching the side of August's face.

"Owwww!" Now it was August's turn to howl. "Brute," he cried, letting Ozzy go.

With a single bound, Ozzy leapt across the floor and on to the top of the crate where Anthony and I were hiding. He looked down through the slats of broken wood and licked his paws.

"He's seen us. Now he's going to eat us," gulped Anthony.

"Ozzy, it's me, Violet. I am not a mouse," I whispered, standing frozen in the glare of the cat's shimmering eyes, which now seemed as big as car headlights.

"I'm your friend, remember."

Ozzy arched his back and hissed.

"I warned you," shivered Anthony, the cobra on his headdress shaking from side to side like a windscreen wiper on a toy car. "Cats are dangerous. This is what I've been dreading all along."

"There's definitely something under that box," said Miss June.

"I don't like it," said Miss July. "Let's get out of here. This place is starting to give me the creeps."

"There's nothing left for us anyway," said August gloomily. "I'm not going near that vicious little tiger to be scratched again."

Out of the corner of my eye I saw him wave his hand towards Ozzy as he kicked a pile of soggy bandages across the floor. "The game's over," he groaned.

"I suppose we better head back to the boat and pretend to be those two sweet little old ladies again," said Miss June.

"Righty-ho," sighed August, putting on his posh Professor Gus voice. "And I'd better be the English Egyptologist."

"At least we've got all that lovely cash we raised from the party," said Miss July. "We did quite well actually."

"Imagine how furious that little brat Violet and her silly old grandma would be if they realized the cats will never get a single penny from their great fancy dress idea," sniggered August.

"I'd love to see their faces when they found out there's no such charity as CLAW," laughed Miss June. "Not unless it stands for Calendars Leave

Astonishingly Wealthy!"

I could feel the blood boiling up from the tips of my toes.

How dare they laugh at us like that.

I wanted to scream and kick the side of the crate. I could hear Anthony breathing heavily beside me. I could tell he was furious too. But we both knew we had to stay statue-still like two stone *shabti* in a museum case or Ozzy would pounce. He held us in his emerald-green stare, his legs bent ready to spring at any moment.

"I tell you something," laughed August. "Mrs Short, that old grandma of Violet's, won't give us any bother for a while. I found her poking around earlier. I gave her a little **push** in the right direction, if you know what I mean."

That did it. I couldn't stay still a moment longer.

"How dare you," I cried, leaping forward, waving my arms.

August couldn't hear me of course. If he could, he would have squashed me with his shoe as if I were nothing more than a bug.

It was stupid of me. The minute I moved, Ozzy pounced.

"Idiot," I heard Anthony hiss.

But then the strangest thing happened.

Instead of clawing or biting, Ozzy grabbed us both gently by the scruff of our necks as if we were two tiny kittens. I could feel his hot breath on the back of my head. He was holding me as gently as a feather.

"Relax, Anthony. He's not going to hurt us," I breathed as

Ozzy bounded forward.

"Look, the cat's got something," said Miss

June. "It might be valuable. I saw a flash of blue

and gold."

It must have been Anthony's pharaoh costume she could see.

She made a dash for him, but Ozzy was too quick. He sprung up towards one of the empty cat holes.

"You're wrong," said Miss July. "I reckon it's a little white mouse. Look at its skinny tail."

I realized that one of my mummy bandages had started to come undone and was trailing out behind me.

Ozzy leapt towards the next cat hole. Higher and higher he sprang, until, at last, with Anthony and me still safe in his jaws, he reached the highest hole of all, right up under the roof.

He stood for a moment looking down on the world beneath him like a mighty Egyptian god.

If the Calendar Gang had been able to see us clearly, they might have thought Ozzy had two little key rings dangling from his mouth, one of a pharaoh and another of a mummy.

But a second later, Ozzy dropped us on to the cold stone floor of the cat hole and sprang away.

"Careful," I cried.

But he was gone.

BOING. BOING. BOING.

In three smooth bounds he was back on the ground.

"Look." I nudged Anthony. Ozzy had seen someone walk into the cavern. Someone he knew and loved.

"Musa," I whispered as Ozzy sprung into his owner's arms.

Our guide was standing in the entrance to the cattery with four tall, strong men from the village. He hugged Ozzy tightly. Then he looked around the cavern, trying to take everything in. I wished I was bigger than a bean sprout, then I could have shouted to him about the Calendar Gang and what they were up to.

Musa cleared his throat. "We found Mrs Short in a deep pit," he said. "Her ankle is twisted but she's going to be all right."

"Goodness! However did that happen?" said August, using his silly, posh Professor Gus voice.

"I'm not sure . . . but I am going to find out," said Musa, looking around at the chaos of cooking pots, bandages and spilled spice mixture. "First I need to find Violet and Anthony. They've gone missing."

Miss June and Miss July were struggling desperately to take off their big black leather aprons.

"Oh dear," Miss June whimpered like a frail old lady.

"So many strange things seem to be going on,"

stammered Miss July, swaying from side to side as if she was so delicate she might faint.

"I've had enough of the Calendar Gang and their play-acting," I whispered.

The angry blood-boiling feeling was rising up from the tips of my toes, like hot water bubbling in a kettle.

POP!

As quickly as a jack-in-a-box springing open, I shot back to **full size**.

WHOOPS!

My feet banged hard against the back of the cat box.

"Ouch!"

Behind me, I heard Anthony let out a tiny scream.

"Sorry," I whispered. I must have kicked him as hard as a donkey. (And Anthony was still only the size of a small carrot, of course.)

"Violet? Is that you up there?" said Musa.

"Yes." I leaned further out of the box. "I've been hiding up here for ages. And as soon as I get down I'm going to tell you everything I've seen."

CHAPTER 25

Before I climbed down from the stone cat hole, I scrabbled around with one hand until I felt my fingers close around something small and solid that I knew must be Anthony.

"Come on," I whispered. I couldn't leave him up here while he was tiny. "There isn't a pocket in this mummy costume but I'll slip you between the bandages and we can climb down safely."

The cat hole was too cramped for me to turn my head and see what I was doing. But, feeling carefully, I opened a gap between two bandages just above my knee and slid Anthony inside. He felt heavier than I had expected but I pulled myself forward, swung my legs out of the hole and began to climb.

"Careful, Violet. I'll fetch a ladder," cried Musa. "Your grandmother has already hurt her ankle. We don't want you doing the same thing."

"I'll be all right. I'm wrapped up in bandages anyway," I laughed. If I'd climbed all the way up to the cat holes when I was tiny, I could certainly climb down now I was full size.

"And I can get down too," said a cheerful Australian voice above my head.

"Anthony?" I gasped, looking up. "Is that you?"

"Course it is," he grinned, leaning out of the

cat hole. He was back to full size now too. But, if he was still up there, what had I slipped into the bandages above my knee?

"Are you OK, Ant? ... I mean, Anthony?" I said as he dropped to the floor beside me.

"Don't worry, Violet," he grinned. "You can call me Ant if you like. I've decided it's a cool nickname after all. Like a hero in a computer game – someone small but *POWERFUL*. Someone who wouldn't be scared of anything ever again ... not even *shrinking*, say."

"That's brilliant, Ant," I whispered, "But if you're here ... then who – or *what* – is this?" I dug into the slit in my bandages and wrapped my fingers around the small shape that was hidden there.

I pulled it out and opened my hand.

Lying on my palm was a small piece of bright, blue stone. It was a perfect *shabti*, carved into the shape of a cat.

"How beautiful." Musa let out a gasp of surprise. "Where did you find that?"

"Oh, just up in that old cat hole," I smiled, trying not to let my fingers shake with surprise.

"Wow! That's better than three old pieces of cracked bowl," laughed Ant.

August rushed forward. "Let me see that. I bet these kids stole it," he said, completely forgetting to speak in his English accent.

"I didn't steal it," I said. "And I am not going to keep it either. It belongs in a museum."

I handed the tiny, smooth figure to Musa.

"It is a wonderful object. I have never seen a *shabti* shaped like a cat before," he said.

"Perhaps you could start a museum here – of things you find on the dig," I said. "You could charge tourists a small fee."

"I know I'd pay to see a beautiful *shabti* like that," agreed Anthony.

"The extra money could be used to look after the stray cats," I said. "You'll already have a good start with what we raised tonight at the fancy dress party."

"You can't take that money," cried Miss July.

"That's our money. I mean CLAW's money," said Miss June.

"No," I said. "That money is *not* yours."

"Not any more," said Anthony.

I stepped forward and pointed to the deep scratch which Ozzy had made on the side of August's face. It looked as if he had a long cat whisker drawn across his cheek. "It seems to me that the Calendar Gang have run into a spot of bad luck," I said.

"It definitely seems things are about to take a bad turn for you," Anthony agreed.

"Someone should call the police," I said, turning to Musa and the men from the village. "I think they'll be very interested when they hear what Anthony and I have to say."

"Interfering little pests," growled August.

"I hate children," said Miss July.

"They're even worse than cats," SNEEZED Miss June.

When we had told the police all that we knew, Anthony and I hurried back to the *Cleopatra* to see Gran.

Signor Sipperetto and Louis L'Amour had carried her back to the boat. She was lying on a sun lounger with her injured leg sticking up in the air.

Tiffany was hovering anxiously nearby. I could tell from the way her frizzy hair was sticking up like a bird's nest, she must have been fast asleep when Lola L'Amour woke her up. I wondered if Tiff would ever recover from the shock ... not of finding out Gran was hurt, but of being seen by a fashion model when she had REALLY BAD hair.

"I know a little first aid," said Signora

Sipperetto, sprinting backwards and forwards with drinks of water and slices of fruit for Gran. She was still dressed up as a long-legged scarab beetle from the party. "But there's not a lot I can do," she said. "There are no bandages in the first-aid kit. Not a single one."

"Ah … perhaps I can help there," I said, pointing to my mummy costume.

At that moment Musa came back to the boat, carrying Ozzy purring in his arms. He told us the Calendar Gang had been arrested and taken to the nearest town.

"The international police have been looking for them for years," he explained. "Ever since they were caught selling a lion's paw at the Colosseum in Rome. They must have got it from some poachers in Africa, but they claimed it was from the time of the ancient gladiators. The Calendars are a notorious gang of tricksters. But thanks to Violet and Anthony, they are going to be locked up for a very long time."

"Hip, hip, hooray," whooped Gran.

"I think I better go and change," I said quickly as the passengers began to cheer. "After all, we need to get Gran wrapped up in these bandages as soon as we can."

My toes were tingling as if they were being pricked with a zillion pins and needles. Rescuing Ozzy, catching the Calendar gang, finding the *shabti* – it had all been too much excitement.

"And I need to reach the next level of **Maze of the Mummy**," gulped Anthony. "Right now!"

We nearly fell over each other as we dashed
towards the stairs.

"See," I whispered, as we ducked down out of
sight. "Life's never boring when you're a shrinker,
Ant!"

ACKNOWLEDGEMENTS

Thank you to the team at Scholastic for all the WONDERFUL things you do – especially Genevieve Herr for her SPOT-ON edits and Rachel Phillips for her BIG publicity. Also Alison Padley for her CURLY-WURLY, WRIGGLY-JIGGLY designs alongside Kirsten Collier's INCREDIBLE pictures, Simon Letchford's last-minute MIRACLES and Emily Lamm's EAGLE-EYED copyedit. Also to Pat, Lexie and Claire at RCW for looking after me REALLY well.

Sophie McKenzie and Julia Leonard – your patience and insights have been AMAZING. And the Kuenzler family are TOTALLY terrific to put up with me at all. I know I am often so busy writing that I forget to wash your socks – thank you.

LOOK OUT
for Violet's other adventures

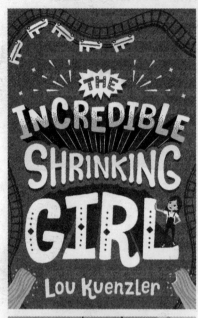